The hymenopterous in nectar he'll be chugging is that of the gods, and only if the doctor agrees with the crew that alcohol and narcotics are the quickest way to recovery from a mild concussion due to a boom boom. The latex antenna should be so lucky.

My job, should I decide to undertake it, as it were, is to determine if the accident was by fault of impaired equipment or that of a preternatural event as the screaming boom operator would have one believe. I vote for a ghost. It makes things infinitely more interesting, or my name isn't Beluga Stein, P.I. —Psychic Investigator. Part-time, anyway. That is, when I'm not teaching biology to a bunch of undergrads who know everything about libido except how to spell it. So my ballot is cast for a ghost.

On the other hand, if Craft Services can't provide something more nourishing than imitation-artificial-processed-cheese-food-substitute, like, say, a decadent chocolate bar, I'm out of here. I have standards.

Wish I could say the same for dear Tanya.

Praise for The Beluga Stein Mysteries

Here's a book with something to please everyone. Thoroughly amusing! — *Chronicle, SF, Fantasy & Horror's Monthly Trade Journal*

Planchette and Beluga Stein are two of the best new sleuths to grace the pages of the mystery novel! — *Spine Tingling Reviews*

Wendy Webb has created an excellent new series of supernatural mysteries that combine great characters with comedy! — C.J. Henderson, author of *The Things That Are Not There*

~*~

Other Books by Wendy W. Webb

Widow's Walk

Bee Movie

by

Wendy W. Webb

The Beluga Stein Mysteries, Book 1

Bee Movie

Cover Art by *The Wild Rose Press, Inc.*

The Wild Rose Press, Inc.
PO Box 708
Adams Basin, NY 14410-0708
Visit us at www.thewildrosepress.com

Publishing History
First Edition, 2022
Trade Paperback ISBN 978-1-5092-4129-3
Digital ISBN 978-1-5092-4130-9

The Beluga Stein Mysteries, Book 1
Previously Published 2003, Marietta Publishing
Published in the United States of America

Dedication

In memory of my grandfather, William Wesley Talbott, who introduced me to Shakespeare and Twain, and made the best bullfrog sound ever.

~*~

Acknowledgements

To Phyllis Boros for telling me, "This book will fly."

Kimberly Hays de Muga made sure everything was where it should be in my manuscript, and provided Bean Burrito Bakes in emergency situations.

I'd like to officially acknowledge David McGregor, a 34-year veteran of the police force for his time and expertise in looking over my police procedural passages. Unofficially, however, I must make note of his sense of humor and disposition for world-class practical jokes.

To Jerri Webb, because she told me I had to put her in the acknowledgements.

The Wild Rose Press is home to the most encouraging, welcoming, and professional people I've ever had the privilege of knowing. But don't tell anyone. I want them all to myself.

Finally, I'd like to recognize all those folks who've experienced the thrill and tedium in making low-budget films. They are a special breed.

Author's Note

Things changed for Beluga Stein since this book first appeared in a different form. Her muumuus of varied floral motifs required a tuck here and there and let out in other places, similar to my words narrating her story.

Supernatural events on the low-budget movie required Beluga's verification, which, by the way elicited her persnickety side at this request.

Tanya insisted on a complete makeover, and Planchette ignored me completely while feigning interest in a dust mote.

If you know Beluga and her story, you might notice a few changes for the better. If you're new to Beluga's exploits (she hates this word preferring instead "adventures", or "daring acts"), welcome.

So get your popcorn, a box of candy, turn down the lights, and get ready. Roll sound. And…action!

Wendy W. Webb

Production Manager's Notes

Shooting on set of Bee Mine delayed yet another day due to unforeseen circumstances of boom falling on antenna of actor playing part of giant bee. Actor sustained minor injury (covered by insurance), antenna sent to SFX department for surgical repair (not covered by insurance), boom operator yet to be found after his exit from soundstage, screaming, "It's a ghost. It's a ghost."

Budget overrun in Craft Services department. Snack Head places blame on Beluga Stein.

Chapter 1

Beluga Stein tugged and shifted the yards of material that made up the muumuu that covered her massive girth. A vivid giant red hibiscus twisted around to drape over one hip, while an anthurium pointed an obscene, yellow appendage at her ample bosom. Rummaging around in her purse—mistaken by many as an overnight bag—she opened a pack of cigarettes, drew out a pastel pink one, and with great fanfare, lit it.

"Thank you, indeed. You are too kind. What's that?" She addressed an imaginary but always gorgeous male companion. Beluga looked around the set of a deserted restaurant and settled on the salad bar prop. "Yes, a real tragedy. Imagine a lovely dinner of," she waved expansively and groped for words, "salad, and the next thing you know, presto-chango, your dream date turns into a real stinger." She inhaled deeply and released a cloud of blue-gray smoke. "No, dear, not stinker, *stinger*. Get it? Bee? Stinger? Guess you had to be there."

Beluga ground out the cigarette in a basket of stale rolls overlooked by the art department at the announcement of the day's wrap. "I was there, and come to think of it, he *was* a stinker. That concussion can do nothing but improve his personality if you ask me. And everyone else involved with this film."

A protesting feline yowl emerged from somewhere in the depths of the salad bar.

"Planchette? Where are you, boy?"

A resonant *whump* on metal, then a scream of razor-sharp claws scrambling for escape pierced the quiet set. Beluga's well-defined eyebrows arched sharply. A solid black round head with pyramidal ears emerged from a circle where earlier a canister held macaroni salad. Vivid green eyes followed. Neither one of them blinked.

"You have celery on your nose."

Clearly bored with the entire experience now, Planchette oozed through the hole and found a tenuous position on the edge to groom himself. He caught sight of the dull plastic sneeze-guard that hung suspended from the top of the bar, swatted at it, then sneezed.

"Right idea, wrong side. But enough dwelling on trivial details. We've got to figure out why there are strange manifestations plaguing this picture." Beluga reached into her purse, pulled out a divining rod that once served as a coat hanger, and scanned it across the perimeter of the set.

Nothing. There was no vibration, not even the slightest of ripples. She snorted, dropped one pointy edge to her ankle to scratch a particularly annoying bug bite, then tossed the instrument into a dark corner. It clattered and settled after a final *sproing*, then assumed the position of abstract art.

So much for household hardware in the realm of metaphysics. One could never trust them to reveal psychic truths. Then again, there was the little matter of bending spoons.

Nah. Too theatrical. And rather hard on the flatware unless one presumed to use them on dinner guests who preferred dysfunctional table manners.

"But you're not like that, are you?" she said to the

imaginary male companion who clung to her every word.

Unlike most of the real males she knew, he listened when she spoke. Besides, it would be eccentric to talk to herself. If only there was a real male in her life right now, someone special to break up the monotony of loneliness. She shrugged, pushed the thought to the back of her mind until it chose to surface at some other inopportune time, and returned to her imaginary companion.

"You, however, have impeccable taste in manners and, needless to say, in women." She puffed up at the statement and leered into the dark. "Of course you do. Now, if I could only bring you to life…"

An overhead light blinked on, shooting dwarfish shadows across the room and cockroaches scattering for cover.

A voice, distinctly male and clearly agitated, assaulted her. "What are you doing here?"

"I'm fine, thank you. And you?"

"I'll call the police if you don't leave."

"And tell them what, young sir?"

She eyed him appreciatively from head to toe. Dark hair pulled back into a ponytail and a handsome face covered with a day's worth of cultivated stubble. His lean muscular body, enhanced by a form-fitting red flannel shirt, disappeared into snug blue jeans that topped well-used hiking boots. Maybe she had brought the imaginary man to life after all.

"Will you tell them that an insubordinate young man tried to evict an old, er, a *woman* who was only here doing her job? Or will they be able to figure that out for themselves?"

"What's your name?"

"Beluga Stein. At this point, I can only guess yours.

Would it be Adonis, and shall I call you Ad, for short?"

His throat tightened as if a painful belch caught there. He swallowed, seemed relieved at the act, then recovered the hardness in his face. "I'm the first A.D. on this film. Assistant Director, in case you didn't know. I keep things moving around here, and I'm moving you outta here."

"I think not, Ad. Hmm. Assistant Director, Adonis, Ad. That works for me. No, dear, I was called in, and I plan to stay. You might say movies are in my blood, at least right now."

Recognition slowly crossed his face. "I remember now. You're—"

"That's right, Beluga Stein."

"The craft services vandal."

"Oh, that. A minor misunderstanding."

"It looked like a bomb went off around the snack cart. Bologna everywhere."

"Baloney."

"Yeah. And chips and candy. It was a real mess. They said you were to blame."

"Baloney. Hooey. Horse hockey." Beluga extracted a blue cigarette, offered the lighter for an act of gentility; he refused then she lit it herself. She inhaled deeply and blew the smoke at an oblique angle past his head. "It's simply not true. I was merely pointing out the lack of nutritional value available and the next thing you know, food fight. It turned out to be a marvelous stress reliever."

"It was a mess. See that it doesn't happen again."

"You're the boss."

"That's right." He turned to leave, then stopped. "You don't really think this picture is jinxed, do you?"

"Jinxed? No. Disrupted? Maybe. Definitely something creepy. I'm just not sure what the affliction is just yet. It's hard to call this early in the game." She pulled a drag from the cigarette and smoothed a wrinkle on her muumuu. "What do you think?"

"Baloney. Hooey." His eyes narrowed to slits. "Horse hockey."

"I see. Succinctly put, if a little crude." She held up her hand to stop his rebuttal effort. "No need to explain further. Besides, you're already late for your date with our star, Miss Blacke."

"How did you…?" He stared at her, then took a step back. "No one knows about that."

"A guess. Call it Beluga's intuition or—"

"Bull—"

"Whatever. Now then, tomorrow's first call is at five thirty, I believe. In the evening, one would hope."

"In the morning, Ms. Stein."

"Heaven help us. Well, a P.I.'s work is never done."

"May it be a short stint."

He turned on his booted heel and left the set. A minute later, the metal door to the soundstage closed with a heavy clang.

"C'mon, Planchette. There's little time left to get our much-needed beauty sleep. I'm speaking primarily of you, of course."

Planchette glared at her, then leaped off the edge of the salad bar to follow.

"Rest for the weary later. Right now, we have places to go and people to meet."

Chapter 2

Beluga rose from her perch on the cement patio bench outside the cafe. Pulling the worn mohair coat tight around her muumuu, she prepared for the impact. "Tanya, darling. So nice to see you."

Tanya launched herself into Beluga. The two women grazed each other's cheeks and kissed the air.

"Beluga! *Compreranno vestiti Maria e Luisa*? Will Mary and Luisa buy dresses? Hello, Planchette. Surly as ever I see."

The cat growled, then promptly ignored her.

"Still studying foreign languages, are we? Italian this time. Any progress?"

"Better luck than with men, I can tell you. Let's see…" Tanya cast her abundant eyelashes down, then pressed a lethal-looking fingernail to the edge of the orange lipstick that rimmed her lips without actually ever touching them. "*Roberto comprerà un regalo per sua madre*. Robert will buy a gift for his mother."

"How lovely for her. Now then, how are you? Really?"

"A widow."

"Again? What does that make? Six?"

"No, sad to say. Seven." Tanya brushed her hand across her face as if erasing away a tear. She frowned. "Bone-dry. There's no more crying left in me for poor, dear Stanley."

"A tragic end, like the others?"

"Washing machine."

"He was cleaned to death?"

Tanya glared. "It's wrong to make light of those who have passed beyond. You, of all people, should know that. Shame on you."

"You're right. I'm sorry. What happened?"

"He chose to go for a walk at the exact moment a wreck of a washing machine was launched from a fifth-floor apartment balcony."

"My God. That's terrible."

Tanya nodded; her voice cracked. "Yes, yes. It was. I can't hear a spin cycle without thinking of him."

Beluga coaxed her friend onto the cement bench and wrapped an arm around her. "I'm so sorry, dear. So very sorry. You must have loved him deeply."

"It was the best six weeks of my life."

"Remind me again. How long had you known him?"

"I met him in the produce section between the instant salad and the matchstick carrots. That night was pure magic. We were married the next morning. Of course, his kids thought I was only interested in his money, but it's not true. It's simply not true." A small smile crept to her lips. "I was far more interested in the cute little mole on his—"

"I get the picture."

"I miss him terribly." Tanya's tone changed to that of a martyr in the throes of great theatrics for a gullible audience. "I'm lost without him. Completely, helplessly lost."

The verbal games had begun, and Beluga was ready for the challenge.

"You mean that expensive sporty number in the

8

parking lot hasn't cheered you up?"

"We all deal with grief in our own way. It's my one extravagance in memory of him. Besides, I got an incredible deal on it."

"I see. Well, one can only hope he's happy in that laundromat in the sky."

"Yes, I suppose you're right. But don't you see? That's why I'm so interested in your work on the movie." She sighed deeply and assumed the best look of calculated vulnerability she could muster. "I have to live my lonely widow's life vicariously through you. There is nothing else left for me. *Nothing*."

"Until the next available male who meets your rigid criteria of, say, breathing, appears on your doorstep."

"Perhaps you could take a lesson, Beluga, dear."

"That's low, Tanya."

"Anyway," Tanya said, completely recovered now, "my dearest friend in the world, whom I haven't seen in eons, breaks away from a leisurely life of perpetual sabbatical as a biology professor to check out strange stirrings in a low budget movie. And out of the blue, I'm invited for an early dinner. Why?"

"Not one to mince words, are you?"

"*Ha messo il sale sulla tavola*? Did you put salt on the table?"

"No. But I tossed a little over my shoulder. Things aren't going well on the set."

Tanya's orange lip ring formed a big, wrinkled "o." She leaned close to Beluga and winced at the cold bench. "Tell me every detail, but tell it quick. It's cold as hell out here. Why *al fresco* in Atlanta in the middle of February? Oh, never mind. Tell. I'm all ears."

"Yes, I can see that."

Tanya ignored her. "You've tried the crystal ball?"

"It's holding the door open to my study."

"The Tarot? It always worked for me."

"Since my last Tarot blackjack game with a doctor of theology, I haven't been playing with a full deck—don't say it. I'm still convinced he's got a card or two up his sleeve."

"Cheeseburger basket," the waitress announced, shivering against the cold.

Tanya raised her hand, then winked at Beluga. "I see you haven't forgotten my eclectic tastes." The paper container, already forming a growing grease stain, plunked down in front of her. "*Fa freddo oggi*. It's cold today. Too cold to sit outside."

"Yeah. Sure is," the waitress said. "There's plenty of room inside if you want. Who got the Veggie Medley on Flower Pot Bread?"

Tanya gasped. "No one at this table."

"That's mine," Beluga said. "Fresh air is good for the soul. So is nutritious food. We'll eat out here. Extra sprouts?"

The waitress offered a tolerant and experienced smile. "Enough to pick out of your teeth for a month. Or until the cheesecake *a la mode*, extra whipped cream, pie on the side, is ready.

"I knew it," Tanya said. "Nutritious food, my ass."

"One must sustain life, mustn't one?"

"Whatever you say, Beluga."

"And finally, a fish plate, hold the fries, hold the slaw, hold the tartar sauce. No bones, no head, no seasoning, but ripe nonetheless, and the oldest one we could find. Are you really going to eat this?"

Beluga reached for the paper plate and set it on the

table. "I'm not, but he is. Come and get it, boy."

Planchette abruptly ended stalking wildlife under the cement patio furniture and leaped on the table for a cursory sniff.

"He's a cutie." The waitress leaned toward them and whispered in conspiratorial tones, "And he's got better table manners than most of the clientele here. Can I pet him?"

Beluga popped a tomato wedge in her mouth. "Sure, but he hasn't eaten in a while, so I'd keep my fingers away from his mouth."

The waitress considered this. "Maybe I'll wait. Well, let me know if you need anything. Oh yeah, I'm supposed to say this: 'I'm Jennifer, and I'll be your waitron today.' Stupid, huh? God, I hate this place." Mumbling under her breath, she disappeared into the building.

"Nice girl," Tanya said between mouthfuls of cheeseburger.

Beluga picked out a sprout that wedged itself between her front teeth. "She'll be okay. A particularly lucrative acting job is on its way."

"How do you do that?"

"Do what?"

"Come up with these predictions? You're always right. Well, sometimes. On occasion anyway."

"I guess I never really thought about it. It's so sporadic, you know. And it seems to happen with a will of its own." Beluga checked on Planchette's progress, then nibbled half-heartedly on a piece of zucchini. "The thought is there suddenly, or I see pictures in my mind. Sometimes the whole story is played out in the pictures. And sometimes it's only a puzzle piece that I have to put together."

"Can you see, say, the soundstage? Right now?"

"Clear as a bell. I can also see the producer walking out the front door."

"You are amazing, Beluga Stein."

"Yes, I am. But not with the clarity you have so easily attributed to me."

"Oh?"

"The soundstage is behind you. Over there, across the street."

Tanya whirled around on her cement seat and dropped a French fry in her lap.

"The young Buddy Holly clone with the blinding white shirt and black tie is our producer, Boley Ash. Better known as 'Ashbole' due to an unfortunate computer error. Wonder what he's up to."

"He's awfully young."

"The family money is much, much older."

"I see." Tanya scooped the fry from her lap and eased it into her mouth. She watched the young producer move toward his car.

Planchette took a breath from his continuous eating, spied the activity across the street, then arched his back and spit.

"Couldn't have said it better myself, boy." Beluga smoothed his ruffled fur and inched the fish plate toward him. "There's something strange in that place, and I'm going to find out what it is."

The producer's expensive, late model car surged to life and rolled out of the parking lot. He accelerated past them without so much as a nod or glimmer of recognition.

Tanya dipped another fry into a mound of catsup, forming ice crystals on its surface, and popped it in her mouth. "Distracted, wasn't he?" She returned to her hamburger and stopped with it raised halfway. "That's why you wanted to eat here, wasn't it? So you could keep an eye on that building. It looks older than dirt."

"A hunch, Tanya. Yet I find that I have little more information than when we first got here."

"But you've got something. So does Planchette, although I must admit I never could understand cat-speak."

"It's Greek to me sometimes, too."

The cat growled softly.

"No offense, Planchette." Beluga wadded up her napkin and dropped it in the paper basket. "Boley hired me to find and fix what seem to be supernatural events annoying this film. Admittedly they were few and could be easily explained away, but there was something else that picked and nagged."

"One of your mind pictures?"

"That and a feeling." Beluga fumbled in her purse for her cigarettes. She chose a sky blue one, lit it, inhaled deeply, then blew out the smoke while explaining. "Drawers opened in the office. Papers were shuffled about when supposedly no one was there. Then there were odd manifestations on the set. New light bulbs shattered before they were turned on. Sets were tampered with enough that the repair crews were more busy than usual. You know, that kind of stuff."

Resting her hand next to the paper food basket, Beluga flipped her lighter on and off. On and off.

Tanya swallowed and shrugged. "Okay, so someone is messing around in the office after hours and is keeping mum about it. Look at that building. It must be a demolition oversight. That would explain the electrical problems."

"Exactly." The lighter went on. It flickered in the light, cool breeze, then went off. "Or the set damage could be the result of a disgruntled cast or crew member. God knows there are plenty of them." She drifted off within herself, deep in thought.

"Or it could all be the result of an unhappy producer!"

"That's what I'm thinking. But there's something else around. I'm almost sure of it."

Something...barely there. It was like a particularly recalcitrant puzzle piece that refused to fit no matter how much pounding one's hand applied to it. Or, in this case, perhaps it wasn't a puzzle but a strip of film that landed on the cutting room floor. The strip was only part of the story, but it could not stand alone as reason for the disturbances. The lighter clicked in her hand. On, off, on, off.

Planchette's head snapped up out of the fish basket to stare across the street. His eyes widened, his ears folded back on the top of his head.

On. A flame from Beluga's lighter set the edge of the crumpled napkin on fire. She didn't notice.

Something was happening, or going to happen. Soon. Something—

"Oh, oh, oh!" Tanya leaped to her feet and frantically shook the bottle of catsup over the flame.

Beluga looked from the flame as it caressed the remnants of Flower Pot Bread to Planchette's stare. "What do you see, boy?"

Tanya yelled and pounded the catsup bottle. "Who the hell cares what he sees? Your food's on fire. Stop asking that cat questions and do something."

A picture formed in Beluga's mind: *A spark touched*

*to oily cloth by...not a hand, but...something. Smoke. Ash.
A ring of ash.*

Tanya coughed and fanned away the small tendril of smoke drifting on the cool wind from the Veggie Medley. "*La mele è un animale*. The apple is an animal." With a snarl, she dropped her hands to her hips. "What am I saying? Well, if you don't care, I don't. I just hope you ordered your muumuu well-done."

A wall of ice water appeared like a tidal wave to drown the ignited food. Ice cubes skittered across the cement table and rolled off the edge.

Beluga blinked and gazed into the eyes of the waitress.

"Food that bad, huh?" she said, holding an empty water pitcher. "It'll be my pleasure to relay this graphic compliment to the chef. Are you all right?"

"Yes, I'm fine, but the soundstage..."

Tanya fanned away drifting smoke and poked at a pickle spear that floated in the water on the table. "The fire is out here, so where is the smoke coming from?"

Planchette shook his drenched feet one at a time but never wavered from his unblinking stare at the sight across the street.

"The soundstage, Tanya." Beluga climbed out from the confines of the cement picnic table and turned to the waitress. "Call the fire department. Tell them to check the storage room in the back. Hurry!" She grabbed her purse and nudged Planchette into motion. "C'mon, Tanya. Let's see if we can stop it before too much damage is done."

"Smoke?" Tanya's voice was small as she stared across the parking lot to the stage. "Fire?"

"That's right. Where there's smoke, there's bound to be fire. Unless we've caught it early enough." Beluga trotted a few steps then stopped. "Are you coming, Tanya? Or do you plan to stand there and regale the patrons of this fine establishment with more clichés?"

Tanya opened her mouth and released the word with every bit of breath her lungs could hold. "*Fire*." Like a bolt of lightning, she shot across the parking lot toward the building.

Beluga rolled her eyes and dropped cash on the table. "Leave it to Tanya to stick me with the bill. C'mon, Planchette. I have a feeling we live in interesting times."

Chapter 3

The door to the soundstage swung open and closed on creaky hinges while releasing billowing white smoke to the cool air outside.

Tanya arrived first. Miscalculating the corner of a brick wall, she collapsed atop an overturned garbage can and erupted in a stream of expletives.

Gasping for breath and holding her sides for fear they would explode onto the pavement, Beluga pointed an accusing finger. "Something…had to…knock the…sense…into you. What were you…thinking about? It could be…dangerous…in there."

Tanya took a deep breath. "A burning building. Maybe someone's in there. I had to do something. I lost my mind, so sue me. Oh no!" She raised a hand to her fluttering, lengthy eyelashes and glared at the havoc imposed on her fake fingernails by the fall. Her voice turned to instant sarcasm. "But now I see the logic behind your statement, and it makes perfect sense."

"For once in your life, you listened to me."

"Right," she said, searching for a stray red talon among the debris. "You go in."

"What are you talking about, Tanya?"

"Beluga, when you're right, you're right. I have my whole life ahead of me. You on the other hand—"

"I don't think I like the way this conversation is going."

Sirens, lots of them, sounded in the distance and grew louder as they banked corners and echoed down highway corridors.

A series of coughs oozed from the smoke-filled warehouse as the rumpled and foam-covered security guard appeared, carrying a spent extinguisher.

"Move over, Tanya. Let Security Bill have a seat on the garbage can." Beluga escorted the large officer over and assisted him to a sitting position. "Raise your hands above your head. That's it. Now take a deep breath, another, and tell me what happened."

"Ms. Stein," he said through a foamy cough. "So good to see you, as always."

Tanya snorted. "Dispense with the platitudes, Bill. Get to the meat of the story."

Security Bill cocked his head at Tanya. "She a friend of yours, Ms. Stein?"

"Depends."

The sirens achieved a deafening pitch as assorted government vehicles careened into the parking lot. The fire marshal screeched to a halt first and jumped from his car, followed by two red fire engines, a neon yellow-green rescue truck, three police cars, an ambulance, a television crew, and a handful of lawyers who sprinkled the lot with European sports cars, top-of-the-line domestic automobiles, and one vehicle made up of junked parts from dozens of other cars that was almost as old as the one Beluga owned.

Notepad in hand, the marshal approached, with an expression void of any ability at levity. "What have we got here?"

Security Bill stood and offered his foam-covered hand, which was refused. "Nothing. It's out. And there's no one in there. They all went home hours ago except for Ashbole. That's the producer. A bit of a toad if you ask me, but I'm getting a raise, so that's neither here nor there."

The marshal was not amused. "Well, we'll see about that."

A team of firefighters clad in heavy gear entered the building cautiously and started their explorations. Flashlight beams skittered across near walls and disappeared into the depths of the warehouse.

A young, handsome lieutenant returned to the door, pushed his helmet back from his forehead, and leaned out. "What the hell kind of place is this anyway?"

"It's a soundstage," Bill said. "We're making a movie."

"So pay no attention to that bee behind the curtain. Or the giant hive prop, or any other hymenopterous paraphernalia you might run across," Beluga said.

The firefighter looked to the marshal. "Is she for real?"

Tanya sidled up to the young man. "No, she's not. But I am. And I just adore men in uniform."

"Hormone alert," Beluga muttered under her breath.

Amusement flickered across the lieutenant's eyes.

"I try to speak several languages," Tanya added.

Beluga snickered. "Subtle, flirtatious English not being one of them."

"And I am memorable in Spandex."

"Yes, dear." Beluga pried Tanya away from the lieutenant's side. "But we try quite diligently to repress some memories. Now let's allow this nice man to do his job. That is if he can ever work again after presenting him with that staggering fashion visual." She paused in thought and turned to the young firefighter. "Check the storage room. I think you'll find an oily cloth as the cause of the event, if not the catalyst."

"Yeah." Security Bill jumped to his feet. "That's exactly where it was. But I put it out. Me and the foam. How did you know that, Ms. Stein?"

"Yes, indeed. I'd like that very question answered as well." The marshal nodded to the firefighter, who ducked inside to merge with the darkness. "Ms. Stein, is it? And a first name?"

"Yes."

"What's that?"

Beluga nodded. "Yes. I have a first name."

The marshal's dark, mirthless eyes met hers. "Perhaps the seriousness of this situation has escaped your notice, Ms. Stein. You have provided information important to this inquiry. Information that it would seem was known only to you before the event occurred. That makes you a suspect, a possible perpetrator, to a very serious crime."

"Is he speaking to me in English?" Beluga asked the diminishing crowd who were drifting back to their assorted modes of transportation. "Or is it just bad television-ese?"

"Perhaps I could be of assistance?" A cadaverous man of indeterminate age shrouded in an ill-fitting mustard yellow suit approached and pressed a dog-eared business card into her hand. "Beasley Banks, Esquire, at your service."

"There's no address on this card."

Beasley Banks, Esquire, shrugged. "I work out of my car. It saves on overhead. Now it would seem we may have a case of slander, unless of course, the allegations are true, in which case—"

Tanya cleared her throat theatrically. "Ms. Stein is psychic; that's how she knew. It's a gift. There, it's all settled. Now, where is that young lieutenant? Time is wasting."

The fire marshal's eyebrows shot up to his hairline.

Beasley Banks, Esquire, carefully removed his card from Beluga's grasp, then loped to his waiting mixed breed car and drove off with a squeal of tires on asphalt.

"Ms. Stein," the marshal said. "Pending the outcome of this investigation, quackery aside, I may have a few questions for you. In fact, you can bet your divining Ouija board on it."

"There he is," Tanya shouted. "There's my darling knight in shining, heavy, fireproof attire."

The lieutenant walked out, blinking in the bright sunlight. "It was a pile of oily cloth too close to a heater. A spark might have touched it off. The whole place could have gone down, as old as it is. The damage is minimal, smoke mostly. So it appears, at least for now, that you're back in the movie business."

The marshal sneered. "I'll expect your full report, Lieutenant. And I want to talk to this Ashbole person." He turned to Security Bill. "Ashbole. What kinda name is that? You got a number where I can reach him?"

"Yes, sir." Security Bill fumbled through the foam, found a pocket, then pulled out a worn notebook. "Right here."

"Good. Walk with me to my car. As for you, Ms. Stein," the marshal said, "I don't take kindly to store-front charlatanism as an attention-getting device. My job is a serious one, and the likes of you people only waste my time."

"You people? Like, say, your aunt with the billboard-size hand on her front lawn touting her gift?" Beluga watched him leave, Security Bill in tow. "And another thing, Mister, uh, fire marshal man, bring your wife red carnations tonight. A large spray. She'll be fine then, you'll see."

His back stiffened. He half turned to look at her, decided against it, and climbed into his car after a cursory discussion with the security guard.

"That was a nasty fight they had," Beluga said. "Poor dear. Mrs. Fire Marshal has her hands full with that one."

The lieutenant sighed. "Tell it. We all do."

Tanya clung to the young man like sticky tape. "I'm a handful, too. Try me tall, dark, and soot-loving."

The firefighter laughed. "You're something else."

Tanya batted her eyelashes and grimaced when one stuck to her skin and sealed her eye closed. It popped loose with the aid of a ragged fake fingernail. "Do you find me attractive?"

"Yes, ma'am," he said with sudden awe and a distracted flicker in his eyes. "You remind me of my grandmother. Haven't seen her in ages. I think I'll call her soon as I get back to the station." He signaled his crew and walked to the fire engine. "I'd forgotten how much I miss her."

The engine backed up with air-shattering, rhythmic siren blasts, lunged out of the parking lot, and disappeared down an otherwise abandoned street.

"Well," Tanya said, smoothing her clothing and brushing away an errant blob of residual foam. "I have never been so insulted in all my life."

Beluga laughed. "Get used to it, Grandma. Besides, there are laws in this state contrary to your intentions.

Here's the man of the hour back again." She waved the guard into the little circle. "So what have you got to say for yourself, Security Bill? It seems you were the real hero today."

The guard approached them, shaking his head. "I don't like it. Don't like it one bit."

"Oh? What's that?"

"Me too old?" Tanya droned. "How dare the little punk. His grandmother. Ha, I say. Ha. Ha."

"Give it a rest. Now then, Bill, what's the problem?"

Security Bill sniffed, tucked his thumbs into his belt, untucked his thumbs to cross his arms, shifted from foot to foot, sniffed again. "The marshal doesn't like you, Miss Stein. I think the hand sign comment did it. Imagine someone not liking you. Just imagine. And someone as fine, as classy a lady, as yourself. It's not right. That's all there is to it."

"I bet the lieutenant's grandmother needs liquid reconstitution so no one will mistake her for dried fruit. Ha. *I*, on the other hand, have skin to die for. Ha. Ha."

"Bag it, Tanya. Go on, Security Bill."

"The marshal wishes he could watch you use your psychic powers to bend the bars of a jail cell. The one you'd share with his aunt if he had anything to do with it."

"I see. Too bad he doesn't. That third eye of his is slammed tighter than vacuum-sealed frozen food. A pine cone could figure out I had nothing to do with the fire."

"I have the skin of a twenty-year-old. And the body. The very idea that I remind him of his grandmother is absolutely—" Tanya raised a hand of mangled fingernails to her open mouth and paled behind her Kabuki-like makeup.

Beluga followed her gaze to the open door of the warehouse. "What is it, Tanya? What do you see? Is Timmy in trouble? Is he in the well again?"

Tanya's voice dropped to a half-strangled whisper. "Something's in there. A shadow. Moving. Something bad."

Chapter 4

Beluga brushed away a blob of extinguisher foam fallen from a disposable and unusually large bee stinger. The flashlight Security Bill had pressed in her hands before the women entered the dark building captured Tanya in a brilliant beam of spotlight white. "So we're in the singed soundstage. Now what?"

Tanya gasped. The little color left in her face drained away in the half-life of the light source. "Oh my God."

Panic gripped Beluga's stomach and twisted. She whirled around in the darkness like a high-speed lighthouse. "What? Where?"

"You girls okay?" Security Bill shouted from his vigil at the door.

"Are we, Tanya?" Beluga swallowed hard and rested the light beam by the corner of the storage room. "Just say we are, and I'll believe you."

"My pantyhose," Tanya whined. "I can feel the hole where my toe popped through. They're my last pair."

Beluga released a long-captured breath through clenched teeth, sucked in another breath, then bellowed, "I'm fine, Bill. Tanya should be so lucky."

"What's that?" Security Bill yelled. "I think I've got foam up one ear."

"Things are great, Bill. Couldn't be better."

"Ten-four, Miss Stein. You know where I am if you need me."

"And they dare to call it 'reinforced toe,'" Tanya snorted. "That's a laugh. Three dollars and ninety-five cents of a laugh direct from the discontinued and mismatched sale bin. What will I do now?"

"Tie a knot in the end and put a sock in it," Beluga snarled.

"A sock in my pantyhose? Isn't that a bit redundant?"

"The sock's for your mouth. Unless you want to tell me what you saw and where you saw it. That was the point for coming in here, right?"

Beluga shot the light beam around the frame of the storage room door. Where flame licked the walls, black fingers of soot inched out around the jamb and crept upward. The smoke had settled, leaving a dusting of fine ash inside and outside the room.

"There." Tanya stamped her foot. "Feels funny. I don't like being all knotted up."

"Neither do I. Only this knot is in my stomach. Something's wrong here. Bad wrong." The flashlight beam scanned the floor inside the room, back and forth, then returned to the doorframe.

"That's what I said. Maybe you'll believe me for a change."

"I believe you, Tanya. It's a sad commentary on my mental health, granted, but I do believe you." The flashlight beam traced a pattern on the floor. "The essence of truth, if little else, is always in your words, but there's nothing like solid proof. Look."

"Great. Just great. The pantyhose knot is wedged between my toes like some kind of geisha girl torture device."

"Look, Tanya!" Beluga froze. "This is definitely not good."

"*Ha comprato il sapone*? Did you buy the soap?"

"No, my dear friend, who has lost her last wit. But I do worry that someone else has bought it if you get my drift." Beluga hiked a yard or two of muumuu material to her thighs and groaned to a squat. "See the line of ash? It follows around this way and all around over there, but the floor is clean in the middle here. Yep, no doubt about it. There was a body here. A strange body. The torso is unusually large, and the head is, to say the least, unusual."

Beluga stood and walked around the body imprint while adopting her best professorial tone. "Most important, the ash is intact. The body was here through the fire. Now it's gone. And if you look closely," she aimed the flashlight beam like a laser, "you will see there is no disruption of the linear ash progression. That is to say, the body did not dance out, mosey out, nor was it dragged. It simply disappeared."

"That's a body I'd rather not meet in a dark building."

"Like this dark building?"

"Thanks for reminding me, Beluga, dear heart. I think I'll just step outside for a breath of—" Tanya's voice turned to a gagged whisper. "Something touched me. My leg. Shine the light. Oh, oh, oh."

The flashlight beam whirled to Tanya's legs.

She screamed. "No. Don't. I've changed my mind. I don't want to see it. If you have any vestige of human good, you'll drag my rigor mortis-ridden body out into the light and get me a strong drink. I'm begging you, Beluga. I'm pleading. Keening might be next."

"There you are, my little love boat," Beluga said. "Relax, Tanya. It's Planchette. I wondered where he'd gotten to."

The cat yowled, brushed against Tanya's legs, then wandered over to sniff the ring of ash.

"That disgusting, flea-bitten, rank fish-eating bag of feline hairballs."

Planchette sneezed. His eyes widened, and his gaze darted from one place in the room to another. The hair from his neck to his tail stood on edge.

"Good boy, Planchette. Keep at it, and sing out when you find something."

"Tuna, fish sticks, turkey and giblets, steak and kidney pie."

"What on earth are you rambling about, Tanya? Can't you see my familiar is hard at work?"

"I'm distracting him since I'd rather not see something that will suck the color right out of my hair quicker than drowning in a bleach bath."

Except for his tail that twitched back and forth like a whip, Planchette stood still as stone and stared.

Beluga followed the stare to the far wall. "What do you see, boy?"

"Fisherman's stew, country buffet, stuffed capons."

The flashlight beam slowly rose on the wall.

"There, boy? I don't see anything."

Higher and higher in a painful, slow crawl, the light revealed a giant beehive prop surrounded by cracks and crevices on the old wall, but nothing else.

"C'mon, Planchette. I'm counting on you."

A creak. A low moan of metal heavy with weight. Planchette crouched, backed up, then stared transfixed overhead.

Beluga aimed the light at the ceiling. "Of course."

"Duck à l'orange, lobster thermidor, fillet of—I think I've lost my appetite." Tanya forced a weak smile then passed out facedown in ash.

"Well, Planchette, it looks like the Bee Man took wing, as it were. Now, what do we do?"

Production Manager's Notes

Body of Bee Man found suspended by SFX flying apparatus, aka an old crane.

Insurance suspended.

Shooting of insect flight scenes indefinitely suspended.

Producer Boley Ash suspends payroll while in jail for suspicion of murder.

Beluga Stein overheard referring to situation as "deep doo-doo."

Beluga Stein's Diary

Ashes to ashes, the Bee Man is but a dusty memory now. And while he may be captured forever in celluloid (which may or may not be seen in a theatre near you), he has left behind far more questions than answers.

The cast and crew have been interrogated exhaustively by officials, but their collective information has produced only one weak thread of knowledge: The Bee Man was indeed a real stinker.

After his concussion, wherein we hoped the Bee Man's personality would improve, it seems he took a nose dive, as it were, in competing for last place in the Mr. Congeniality award by threatening Boley Ash. What exactly took place is still unknown since no one has been able to talk to the young producer since his incarceration.

The idea of questioning Boley is a personal challenge of the highest magnitude, and I am making plans accordingly. I will get to him even if it means scaling prison rock walls, jumping over razor wire, bribing prison officials, or the very real chance of forever waking up with "Jailhouse Rock" running a continuous loop through my brain.

Sometimes one must take the bad with the good.

In the meantime, the body of the hymenopterous actor was lowered from the SFX crane and taken away by an unusually large stretcher able to contain the impressive but damaged costume and unrecognizable body for further study by the Medical Examiner's office.

In the seat next to the ambulance driver was the retrieved broken antenna, denuded of most of its latex. Placed diagonally and jutting out of the window at an acute but rather limp angle, the antenna had the unique ability to transmit low radio frequencies.

Special effects people have a strange sense of humor.

Production of the film is on hiatus until the shock wears off, or the maintenance people vacuum the soundstage of debris. Whichever comes first.

Mostly though, I fear for my dear friend, Tanya. Emerging from the ash looking like a coal miner hobbyist, her pantyhose a chaos of runs and holes, but the knot firmly in place between her toes, she was an exercise in master swooning. My fear was that it was not her usual theatrics but a deliberate attempt to determine if regaining full consciousness was a good thing. She decided it wasn't and was thus ushered off to a nearby hospital for observation.

Perhaps a bee man passing to the other side is not for everyone. Dabbling in the realm of preternatural events is a special vocation, one that warrants screening phone calls before picking up. There's always more there than meets the ear. And other senses.

But first, one must examine the crime to determine if it's a more typical murder or if it's something outside the ordinary. A body found housed in a bee suit and hoisted into the air by a crane definitely falls into the category of extraordinary. Not to mention just plain strange. Thus, it is under these unusual circumstances that one may, indeed must, consider alternate dimensions.

Of course, there is the little matter of the note.

The production staff had thoughtfully provided me

with an apartment for the duration of my stay. *Truthfully, the place was more an archeological dig than a suitable residence, even for those with less than discerning tastes, but it's the thought that counts.*

Anyhoo, found on the bottom rack of my refrigerator was an interesting note leaning against the chocolate chip cookie dough. Or, perhaps, one should say, it was more an interesting visual medium rather than a simple note. Cut-out pictures from magazines, newspapers, and books formed a rather inaccurate picture of a bee man, but the gist was there.

And while the decoupage legs were memorable, an athlete in one of those underwear ads, if memory serves, one wonders when the picture arrived and if it had anything to do with the electricity to the refrigerator grinding to an irreversible halt at that same moment.

P. S. My research has indicated that apartment maintenance does not respond to 911. But then again, no one would in this part of town.

So, as I had mentioned to my dear friend, Tanya, as she was wheeled away on a stretcher, I'll start with unobtrusive questioning and observation of the cast and crew.

Dear, dear, Tanya found high amusement at my use of the word "unobtrusive." Perhaps it was due to shock at the recent turn of events that warranted an outburst on her part. Personally, I believe it was the oxygen. A mask large enough to accommodate her fake eyelashes was strapped to her face and probably delivered more than she was used to getting. Thus her ridiculous grin punctuated by mirthful cackling and snorting.

Or maybe it was the drugs.

Chapter 5

Jett Blacke opened the fishing tackle box, dipped her hand in, and pulled out an impressive collection of mascara wands that covered a spectrum of colors. She peered myopically at each one, then squinted in such a way that her upper lip slid over capped teeth so bright they could cause retinal damage to unsuspecting viewers. Reluctantly she slid a pair of tortoise shell green glasses on the bridge of her mildly hooked nose.

A knock sounded on the trailer door. "Six-thirty. They need you on the set, Miss Blacke."

She ripped the glasses off her nose with the speed of lightning and peered at the closed door. Strands of black hair weighted with hot electric curlers sent blistering heat bouncing around her neck. "Ouch. Tell 'em to wait. Ouch."

A pause. The kid messenger cleared his throat. "Uh, I told them that an hour ago."

"Tell 'em again. I'm not ready. Ouch." She pulled her robe tight, rubbed one calf with a foot covered in a bunny bedroom slipper, and waited.

Silence for a minute, two.

She slipped the glasses back on and rummaged in the tackle box for eyeliner. Green, blue, black, violet, or red to match her eyes after a sleepless night. Damned low-budget movies.

First, it was unavailable professional makeup people

and a part-time costumer who dressed actors in thrift shop rejects. Then, in a blatant attempt to throw salt in her wounds, it was Betty. The film editor suddenly appeared on the job as an unpleasant blast from their childhood past.

Right now, however, the latest insult was a high school kid with Hollywood aspirations and a title that allowed him the privilege of disrupting her sanity before dawn. He coughed outside the trailer door.

"Are you still there?" she said with her best snarl.

"Yes, ma'am."

"Go away."

"I can't do that."

"Force yourself."

"If it were up to me, you could stay in there all day. But it isn't up to me, and I really need this production assistant job."

"Get lost."

His voice changed to a whine. "Atlanta can be kinda cold in February, and the bathroom in the soundstage doesn't work too good. Can I come in for a sec?"

"The bathroom? *My* bathroom? Do I look like a public washroom?"

The trailer door exploded open, and the kid sprawled back a step. Jett lunged down a metal step covered in ice, slipped into a folded heap on the asphalt parking lot, and was batted in the head by the trailer door that finally slammed shut behind her.

"Oh God, not my hair. My makeup. Look what you've done, you little snot. You've ruined me."

He reached out to offer her a hand, and she slapped it away. "See that star on my door? It would imply, to those who have an IQ greater than toast, that I am a person of some importance."

"But—"

"So cough in a refrigerator and grow a life." She rose, checked for bodily damage, then focused her attention on the kid who seemed to have turned to stone with a smirk fixed solidly on his face. "Scram."

He did.

She dusted off her hands, reached for the door, and stopped with the sight. The star had been carefully carved and altered into the shape of an outhouse crescent moon. Her lips curled into a new snarl.

"How appropriate, and so very, very funny." She yanked at the door, ripped a fingernail off at the quick, and yanked again amid a flurry of expletives.

Locked. The door was locked.

It figures.

The muscles in her face rippled independently of one another. A low guttural growl started in her throat and met the cool pre-dawn Georgia air with a bellow like that of a frustrated wild animal. Head bent low, she stalked across the parking lot, shoved open the door to the soundstage, and dared anyone to appeal to her senses.

Ad saw her first. He shrugged, tucked his hands deep into the pockets of his blue jeans, and called out: "Gig, I believe this one's for you."

A petite, attractive woman of Asian descent pressed through the growing crowd. The ski bib overalls she wore to curb the chill of the unheated soundstage rasped with every step, then fell silent as she stood inches away from the towering female lead.

Jett feigned hearing the muffled dialogue of awe ripple through the crew at the director's arrival. She raised her chin and looked down her nose as the expectation of verbal nuclear fallout tightened the group so that no one would miss a word. Their interpretation of the event was sure to escalate anyway and vary as actual facts never stood in the way of a good story, so she would simply act as if none of it mattered.

Gig's voice was low, even, controlled, and capable of bringing a rowdy beer hall brawl to an immediate halt. "Nice of you to join us, Jett. We're ready for a lighting check for the bedroom scene now."

"I'm not ready."

A collective gasp traversed the group.

Gig never blinked. Her well-modulated voice dropped to a level forcing the crew to lean in closer and was delivered with clenched teeth void of perceptible lip movement. "Perhaps the heat surging through your hair has caused a circuit overload in the two brain cells you have left, and you didn't understand me the first time. Assuming this line of thinking is correct, I will repeat myself. *Once*. Lighting check. Bedroom scene. *Now*."

All gazes shifted to Jett for a response

She glared at them, was cheered to see a small recoil, then turned a broad smile on the director. "Of course, Gig. All you had to do was send someone after me, and I would have been here in a split second." She walked through the crowd that parted like the Red Sea for Charlton Heston, mumbled something under her breath to the kid production assistant that turned him instantly anemic, and headed to the set.

"Brava, brava." Beluga applauded wildly. "DeNiro couldn't have handled it better. I loved every minute." She offered her hand to Gig. "Beluga Stein. I was here yesterday."

Gig accepted the handshake without emotion. "Yes, I

remember. Our illustrious and now incarcerated producer hired you."

"Indeed he did. I plan to visit him today."

"He also hired Jett Blacke."

"Because of her talent?"

"A family obligation."

"I'm sorry."

"So am I."

Beluga shrugged. "It looks like you've learned to handle Jett."

"What's the adage? 'Familiarity breeds contempt'? After knowing Jett for what's been a short time but seems like decades, I could have coined the phrase."

"Maybe Miss Blacke's disagreeable behavior is the result of grief," Beluga offered. "The Bee Man's death last night was a shock to all of us."

"Jett Blacke doesn't respond to grief. She doles it out."

"I see."

"And the rest of us don't have time to dwell on unfortunate events." A forced smile crossed her lips. "But I'm being rude. It goes with the territory. The name is Gigi Liu. Gig for short, with a hard G, or you take your chances with physical harm."

"I detest physical harm."

"Good. So do I, for the most part. Coffee?" She led Beluga to the snack cart, pushed the button on a large plastic thermos, and steaming liquid gushed into a Styrofoam cup. "Here. It's not great, but it'll do. Sugar and cream are over there. Donuts, too—"

"I *love* donuts. One of the basic food groups in my book. Very nutritious."

"I hear the rest of our food doesn't meet your

38

nutritional standards." Gig filled a cup for herself, black, and downed half of it in one swallow.

Beluga deposited four packs of sugar and a generous bolt of cream in her cup then sipped. "Word gets around."

"We spend twenty hours a day together. Sometimes more. Nonunion rules. There are few secrets. Tell me all about yourself while we walk to the set. That'll give us about a minute and a half. It's all I can spare right now. Even a death can't stand in the way of a tight shooting schedule."

Beluga was Beluga's favorite topic, and she relished the opportunity but was disappointed in the minimal amount of time allowed her hobby. "Okay, I'll talk fast. I'm here to see if the series of problems this film has had lately is related to some otherworldly event."

"You've done this before?"

"Once, but that's another story."

"Once?"

"It's more than most people."

"Yes, I suppose."

A giant beehive prop sat sullen in a dark corner of a waiting set.

Beluga eyed it with suspicion. "Of course, I've dabbled in metaphysics for many years. You might say it was a sideline science interest of mine. Cigarette?"

"Don't smoke. 'Sideline science interest,' Mrs. Stein?"

"Ms., but call me Beluga. I'm a professor of biology on sabbatical from a small North Georgia college, and this is just a little something to do while I decide on…something else."

"You don't like teaching?"

"I love teaching. It's the fundraising, the paperwork,

and the administration's policies I'm not too fond of."

"I see."

"Do you, Gig? That's good to know. Few see, and even fewer believe. In the metaphysical realm, I mean. Which one are you?"

"I'll let you know." She barked an order at a crew member leaning against a lighting tree, then continued, "Beluga is an unusual name. What is the origin?"

"My parents. A honeymoon cruise in the Mediterranean. Too much champagne and caviar, then nine months later, the rest, as they say, is history. Which reminds me, have you ever received a picture composed from newspapers and magazine cutouts?"

"One. I figured it was a joke by someone who had more time than comedic ability."

"And…"

"And I ignored it. I can ignore a lot of things when I need to. Here we are. Look, Ms. Stein, er, Beluga. Do whatever hoo-doo you do so well, but keep it behind the cameras and out of the way of my crew. Do that, and we'll get along just fine. Got it?"

"Got it."

"Good. Ready to shoot this scene?" A whine rose from the set. "Someone get those hot rollers outta Jett's hair, slide a negligee over her, and deep-six the bunny slippers. Where's the bee?"

Ad spoke into a walkie-talkie. "We're ready for the bee stand-in."

A crackle and sputter of static came back. "On his way."

Seconds later, a man wearing pajama bottoms and a backup bee thorax and head with one antenna missing stumbled onto the set and climbed into bed.

Gig looked through the camera, mumbled direction to the cinematographer, Rick, and walked to the bedside. "Get in, Jett, and pretend you're enjoying this. It's called acting. Okay Bee Man Two, where's your other antenna? Ad?" she bellowed. "What's the story on this costume?"

"SFX is working on it," he said. "We weren't counting on needing a spare bee suit."

Gig rolled her eyes. "I had to ask. Well, Bee Man Two, it looks like you're gonna have to roll over on one side, so we don't see the missing antenna. Yeah, just like that. Closer, you two."

"Flashing." The script supervisor pushed a button on her instant camera that sent a blinding light through the set, then retreated to her chair to examine the developing results.

"Okay," Gig said, "I think we're ready. Beluga, honey, step back a little further. Further. More. Good."

Beluga sidestepped a series of lethal-looking electrical cords that threatened a hip fracture if one were not careful and found a small window of visibility under the focus puller's armpit.

Ad screeched into the walkie-talkie. "Quiet, everyone. We're shooting." His words repeated on communication devices all over the building like a perverse echo.

A bell burst forth with a loud shriek and, Beluga conservatively estimated, took ten years off her life.

"We're rolling."

"Speed."

"And…action."

Jett caressed the bee's chin. "Are you in the mood? I am."

The bee shook his head in the negative.

"Don't you find me attractive anymore?"

Beluga snorted. The script supervisor turned and put a finger to her lips.

"Things don't have to be…" Jett pouted. "Different. Just because they are." Her hand traced a line down the bee's thorax. Her voice turned throaty. "I want you. Now."

A small mound of blanket at the foot of the bed shifted, then slowly rose.

"You want me, too. I can tell."

The bump inched toward the head of the bed.

"Ooh. Yes. You *do* want me."

The blanket bump popped up to twice its original size.

"You…want…me?" Jett's eyes widened. Then slowly, so very slowly, she raised the edge of the blanket and stared. Her mouth opened in a scream that was delayed in coming but was everything she could have hoped for if planned.

"Cut!"

Jett leaped out of bed like she'd been stung. "What the hell?"

Bee Man Two twisted in panic and latex and flung himself off the side of the bed. A black tail writhed like a trained cobra along the edge of the sheets.

"Planchette!"

The cat launched himself like a shot fired from a high-powered rifle and skidded across the cement floor to disappear around a corner.

Gig turned to the cinematographer. "Did you get it, Rick? All of it?"

"Sure did."

"Print it. We'll get Betty to edit out the cat later." The

director smiled to herself and nodded. "I like it. Like it a lot. As for you, Ms. Stein..." Beluga stopped in her escape to recover the cat. "I'd prefer it if your cat pursued his career on his own time."

"He was good, wasn't he?"

Gig cringed at the pitch Jett was taking in her histrionics. "Better than most. He did Jett an acting favor; she just doesn't realize it yet. But please, keep him away from future shots."

"Aye, aye, Captain." Beluga fled in pursuit of Planchette.

Ad, the assistant director, ran to Jett and tried to calm her. The star was having nothing of platitudes or consolation and escalated her tantrum to that of an experienced four-year-old. Her feet stamped and trampled cords and wires snaking across the floor of the set. A loop of wire suddenly rose like a cobra.

She cried out in anger and frustration, spewing four-letter words that would curl hair more effectively than any hot roller, then stopped mid-shriek. In stunned surprise, she watched the wire snare her foot.

The sudden quiet caught the crew's attention, and they, too, watched with a mixture of shock, awe, and an unsophisticated observation of physical law being broken.

A thicker cord twisted around Jett's ankle and tightened. She stumbled and fought to maintain balance.

Gig shouted orders that propelled and sent the crew into a Keystone Cop frenzy. "Cut the juice; pull the plugs; flip the circuit breaker. Someone get her foot out of there!"

"It's creeping up her leg now," Ad yelled.

Jett whined, "Oh God, oh God, oh *God*."

The director spewed rapid-fire orders. "Call the

medic; call the insurance company. Hell, call the fire department and get Beluga Stein back here if we have to. But cut the damn juice *now*."

Lights blinked then went out.

"Juice out," someone shouted from the dim recesses of the set.

Ad clawed at the cord climbing up Jett's leg. "It's still moving. I can't get hold of it."

"Oh God, oh God, oh *God*."

Another voice. "I found the end. Jeez, it's not even plugged in. Never has been. It's dead."

"No," Ad bellowed. "It's alive."

Blinding light from someone's headlamp winked on.

Standing as still and as white as a marble statue, Jett whimpered, then pleaded, "Help me. Please!"

Production Manager's Note

Shooting of Jett Blacke's scenes postponed indefinitely. Actress is locked in trailer and states she will emerge when "Hell freezes over" or her lawyer calls. Whichever happens first. Jaws of Life used to open trailer door (coverage by insurance canceled), but actress refuses to leave.

Production Assistant treated for minor bite wounds (covered by a non-stick gauze pad and a signed health treatment waiver).

Beluga Stein ordered to fix jinx problem, or she will be placed under Craft Services division of Garbage Removal. She has chosen instead to see producer Ashbole at the county jail ASAP.

Chapter 6

Approximately two blocks behind the Georgia governor's mansion, as the crow flies, was an equally impressive dwelling. Beluga stood outside the front door and whistled appreciatively at the façade and carefully manicured lawn. "This is some place."

Hoisting a huge bag over her shoulder that writhed and wriggled, she inhaled deeply from a lavender cigarette, then blew out smoke from her nostrils. "Stop squirming, Planchette. I don't want to repeat that ugly scene with the X-ray machine at the county jail."

She dropped the butt, ground it out under the toe of her faux alligator boot then kicked the cigarette under a Chinese pot holding an ornamental juniper shaped much like a newly groomed poodle.

"I didn't like the way that jail supervisor looked at me. Not one bit. Imagine him thinking I walked around with a bag full of cat bones. They were intact and sleeping, mind you, but bones nonetheless."

Beluga reached into the shoulder bag to stroke Planchette's head. "You did the right thing when you bit him if you ask me, but there really was no need to have all those guns drawn at one time."

Pressing the doorbell once, the alien communication notes from *Close Encounters of The Third Kind* rang out.

"Who knew our illustrious producer had already been sprung by his family's high-powered attorney?"

The massive front door eased open, revealing a dour man in a black suit who announced, "May I help you?" in tones clearly indicating he would prefer to do anything but.

"Yes, you may." She opened the bag. "Stop wiggling, Planchette. I'm here to see Boley Ash."

The man maintained an expression comparable to the fluidity of stone. "Who may I say is calling?"

Beluga looked over his shoulder, then around him. "Amazing. Have you considered a future in ventriloquism? I never once saw your lips move, and I was watching. Do it again."

Eyes fixed and bored, his face was a picture void of any sign of mirth. Or life.

"All right. Fine. We'll play it your way. My name is Beluga Stein; I'm here to—"

The door closed solidly. The latch was thrown.

"Well, I never." She lowered the bag off her shoulder and released the black cat. "Try the juniper, Planchette. I want to leave a little something for Cheeves to remember us by."

The door opened suddenly. The man stepped aside. "You may come in, Ms. Stein. Mr. Ash can be found in the game room. Third door on the right."

"Past the fountain, screening room, and the library."

The barest flicker of surprise traversed the man's eyes.

"It's a gift." Beluga stepped into the marble foyer. "C'mon, Planchette. You'll have to fertilize the plant later. Right now, we have work to do."

Her boots tapped a staccato beat across the checkerboard flooring when she stopped and turned to the manservant. "You might want to see someone about that stomach problem. In the meantime, watch out for spicy foods and keep a stiff upper lip."

His eyes widened.

"Oh, sorry. You already do the upper lip thing. My mistake. Planchette, leave the bird topiary alone." She turned on a sharp heel and went in search of Boley Ash.

The sounds of pings, clicks, and grunts of frustration met her at the door to the game room.

Boley Ash's thin black tie dangled from his neck like an ineffective noose. It swayed in short bursts across the wrinkled white shirt spattered with pizza sauce while he rocked and battered the pinball machine. After pounding the top of the machine, he stared with his good eye at the "Game Over" message scrawling across the screen. His Buddy Holly-type glasses, sans one arm and with a piece of adhesive tape wrapped around the bridge, dipped precariously to one cheek. Righting them as best he could, he turned to Beluga.

"The people in that jail are animals. No, not animals. Animals are too good for them. They should spend the rest of their lives trying to be animals."

"Yes, I've heard that. Shouldn't you put something on that eye? It's terribly swollen."

"They're the fleas on animals. No, not fleas. The stuff on fleas. The stuff fleas make."

"Flea poop?"

"Yeah. Flea poop. That's what they are."

"So what you're saying is they represent the most shallow end of the gene pool."

"Yeah. What?" Boley's glasses launched themselves down one side of his face again. "Whatever." He dabbed at his swollen eye and winced with the pain. "I need a drink."

A button by the door was pushed, and instantly the manservant appeared.

"A cola for me. Make it a double. Do you want anything, Beluga?"

"No, thank you. But Planchette could do with a little water."

Recovered and even more controlled now, the manservant addressed Planchette. "Imported or domestic, sir?"

Planchette swatted the air halfheartedly.

Beluga translated. "Surprise him."

The man backed out of the door, pulling it closed as he went.

"Now about that eye, Boley. You need to put something on it."

"I've got something." He picked up a plastic bag covered with an imported Irish linen napkin and eased it over his eye. "Steak *tartare*. It was the best thing Mumsy could find." Boley sat down in a beanbag chair covered with appliquéd action figures and gently inched the *tartare* bag toward his eye. "Mumsy says this is all a bad mistake, and someone will pay. Father is calling every Supreme Court judge he knows. Too bad there are so many Democrats, or this thing would be over by now."

"That's life in the fast lane."

The manservant reappeared as if on little cat feet.

"Oh, here we are. Thanks, Miles. He's fast, isn't he?"

"Lightning could take a lesson."

Miles placed a tray heavy with soda next to Boley then slid a used plastic butter bowl filled with water toward Planchette. "I chose domestic in keeping with his inbreeding. I'm sure you understand."

Planchette bared his teeth and hissed.

"I catch your drift," Beluga said, nodding toward the cat. "And he does, too. But don't worry, Miles. Planchette's bites get infected and cause skin sloughing or amputation so rarely; it's hardly worth worrying about. Miles? Miles? Oh, my. I'm afraid we scared off that nice man, Planchette. Keep up the good work. There's a little fish treat in my bag there if you want it." Beluga cleared her throat. "Or you can attack the butter bowl. Your call. Now then, Boley, I'm here to do what you hired me to do. Namely, to determine what's causing all the problems on the set. I suppose it goes without saying that things have gotten a little more sticky than we first thought."

Boley downed his cola in one long swig, wiped his mouth with the back of his hand, grimaced, then belched. "They fingerprinted me like a common criminal."

"Yes, they do that. But rest assured you're far from common."

"Tell it."

"Ego aside, Boley, I don't believe you killed the Bee Man."

"'Cause I didn't."

"It's just a feeling I have, mind you, but I trust those feelings."

"I didn't kill the Bee Man."

"Hold off on the editorial, Boley. I'm on a deducing roll. Right now, it's anyone's guess who, or what, killed the Bee Man, but it wasn't you."

"It wasn't me."

"I'm sure that's true. Still, an unanswered question remains. Was the murder caused by a person, or could it have been an entity of some sort?"

"They took my picture while I was in jail. It looks even worse than my driver's license. And then the flea poops beat me up."

"I can see that. So I need to know the details leading to your arrest. What were you doing on the set before the fire, and why did the Bee Man threaten you?"

Boley downed another soft drink and swayed ever so perceptibly as if he were on the road to intoxication via a carbonated soda binge. "Jett Blacke."

"Our narcissistic star? I don't think I quite follow you."

"I think he had a thing for her."

"A thing?"

"The hots."

"Oh, dear."

"I stood in the way, or at least he thought I did. And he always liked to call the shots. He was kinda bossy that way." Boley leaned back in the beanbag chair and slid the *tartare* over his puffy eye, then moaned. "Jett Blacke doesn't even know I'm alive."

"You are, however. The Bee Man should be so fortunate." Beluga wedged herself into a hard plastic chair shaped like an open hand and, for a fleeting moment, wondered if she would ever escape its tortuous grasp. "What did the Bee Man threaten to do if you didn't, er, lay off Jett Blacke?"

"He said he'd torch the place. Ruin the picture and my future in films. I think he wanted a bigger part, too." Boley threw the *tartare* off his face and stalked over to the regulation-size pool table. "Wanna play Eight Ball? I'll break."

"It's been a while. Oh, what the hell. But if this chair grabs me in an unseemly place one more time, it better buy me dinner." With a rude sucking noise, Beluga extricated herself from the hand, smoothed her muumuu of swaying palms at dusk then walked to the far wall to scrutinize the pool cue choices. Finding one that met her criteria, she turned to the pool table and watched Boley make a weak break.

A ball tottered at the edge of the corner pocket then fell after he slammed his body into the table.

"Stripes," he said. "That makes you solid."

"Some might argue with you there." She chalked the end of the cue. "How was the Bee Man going to ruin your future in film?"

"I don't know. He was kinda vague on the details. Fudge. Look how close I was. I guess it's your turn."

"That one, straight, corner pocket." Beluga tapped the cue ball, watched it meet a solid that landed with a resounding *whump* in the designated pocket. Studying the table for appropriate geometry, she pointed at another solid with the cue. "And that one, banked here, then there, into the side pocket."

The move was executed as planned, and the ball disappeared.

"Why didn't you just fire the Bee Man and get him off the picture and the lot? Solid, this corner pocket."

It dropped easily and rumbled through the inner catacombs of the table.

"You've done this before," Boley said, with the beginning of a whine.

"Actually, I'm kinda new at the murder biz."

"I meant pool."

"Oh. That. I've played a time or two. Never really understood the game, but it seems simple enough." She slid the cue behind her, leaned at an unnatural and exhibitionist angle, caught the sad puppy dog look in Boley's good eye, and threw the shot. "Whoops. Your turn."

"Finally. I was afraid you wouldn't let me win like everyone else does."

"Well, now that I know the rules... You didn't answer my question, Boley. Why did you keep the Bee Man on?"

"He said he'd hurt me and Jett. That the plans were already in the works. He called it a domino effect or something like that."

"All because he was in lust with Jett Blacke? It hardly seems worth it."

Boley paused to lean against his upright pool cue. "She's something, isn't she?"

"Indeed. Just what, I'm sure I wouldn't say in polite company. What about Ad?"

"The assistant director? What about him?"

"How does he feel about all this amorous attention directed at Jett?"

"Nothing. He doesn't even like her. Everyone knows that." Boley's good eye narrowed in suspicion. "Unless you know something, I don't."

"Many things, I suspect. But little having to do with this situation."

"That's okay then." He flung the pool cue away and positioned himself in front of a video game monitor. "Remember, I'm still the boss. Even if the Bee Man didn't believe it."

"My memory isn't that bad." Beluga retrieved her purse, extracted a goldenrod-colored cigarette, and lit it.

"Mumsy says cigarettes are filled with rat droppings and carbon monoxide."

"Good." Beluga inhaled deeply then blew out a series of smoke rings. "I could use the protein and a rosy glow in my cheeks." She ashed in the plastic pouch belonging to a toy Quasimodo. "What were you doing on the set before the fire started?"

"A little paperwork. That's all."

"Did you start the fire on the stage, Boley?"

There was no answer except tiny electronic beeps from the video game.

"Boley?"

"Why would I want to start a fire?"

"Things weren't going your way. The picture was behind schedule. Everyone called you Ashbole. Any number of things."

"I hate that name. Max hates it, too."

Planchette stopped his systematic destruction of the butter bowl and turned wide eyes on Boley.

Beluga stopped inhaling mid-draw. "Max? Who is Max?"

"Someone. Something." He turned off the game. "Never mind. It isn't important."

"It could be, Boley." She paused and looked at him carefully. "Tell me about Max. Is he a friend of yours? Another disgruntled member of the film industry? What?"

"I don't want to talk about it anymore."

"But—"

His voice rose, tightened. "Didn't you hear me?" His hands clenched into fists. "I said no more talk."

All the lights in the room suddenly winked off.

Boley sat still and looked deep into the dark, empty video screen. "No more."

Beluga glanced about. "Electrical problems? In a place like this?"

"It happens sometimes. I don't think about it anymore." He relaxed a notch and loosened his fists.

The lights surged immediately back to life then.

He traced a smiley face on the lifeless video screen. "I think you should leave now."

"Are you sure?"

"I'm sure."

"I still have some questions. Like what you may know about pictures cut out from magazines and distributed about as messages. Anything you'd like to add?"

He didn't answer.

"And I'd love to find out more about this Max person."

"No."

"Nothing?"

"*No.*"

The lights flickered but stayed on this time.

"Okay. But you should know I don't give up easily when it comes to being nosey." Beluga swung her bag over her shoulder. "Oh. About the movie. Is it still on?"

"We start back tomorrow."

"Is that wise?"

"I'm on a budget and a schedule. If this movie isn't finished, and a small profit made from distribution, I start work in my father's corporate mailroom the following week."

"C's and D's in business school?"

Boley turned to her. "How did you know that?"

"A guess. What would Buddy Holly do in this situation?"

He straightened the limp tie around his neck and sat up a little taller. "I only wish I knew."

"You'll figure it out. Planchette, I think you've done all the damage to that butter bowl you can. We're leaving."

She drifted to the door. Her familiar followed until he got distracted by another object.

"Beluga?"

"Yes, boss?"

"Please don't let them send me back to jail."

"I'll do my best. Planchette! That's a computer mouse. Honestly."

"And don't miss your mark."

"My mark?"

Boley offered his first smile of the day. "I made all the arrangements. You're going to be in pictures. Six a.m. call."

"Oh, God."

Chapter 7

Jett Blacke raised her hand for attention and was completely ignored by the busy film crew. With no choice left, she resorted to her most noted attribute: volume.

"Hold it, you fruitcakes," she bellowed. "Stop what you're doing right now." Her voice cranked up two or three-decibel levels at their continued inattentiveness. "I said, *stop*."

Frantic activity slowed to rumbles, mumbling, then silence as everyone stared at her.

"That's more like it. A few moments of silence is all I ask."

"For the Bee Man?" a lone, unidentified voice asked.

"God, no," Jett said, tossing her head and running her fingers through her hair as if she were in some beauty product commercial. "I need to memorize these lines before we shoot the scene, and there's just too damn much racket going on in here."

Eyebrows raised all around. Lips curled into grimaces.

"Someone get my makeup mirror. It's in my trailer behind the carob-covered malted milk balls. I think I need a touchup."

Ad mumbled into his walkie-talkie. The word "airbrush" ricocheted on radios throughout the building.

Jett debated whether or not she should destroy her new lover at this infraction of undermining her. She could easily muster a barrage of words that would bring him to his knees and make him incapable of walking, or worse, ever again. Catching the warning look on his face, she opted for a pout and adopted the best extended lower lip pose she could produce. "Ad, honey, can I talk to you for just a moment?"

He glanced over his shoulder at the spectators, cleared his throat, and came to her. "We're on a tight schedule, Jett. Don't make me pull rank again."

"That was last night, sweetie. And I loved every torrid military-game moment of it. But now it's business." She ran her finger up and down his chest. Lip quivering just perceptibly, her voice turned husky and deep. "Undermine me again, and I'll cut you off. Now you wouldn't want that, would you? Of course not. Tonight will be the best yet." Her hand slid to the rump of his jeans.

He gasped.

"There now. It's settled." She addressed the gaping crowd. "Quiet on the set, please. This is the Great Aunt scene, and I want it to go well. Otherwise, our illustrious film editor, Betty, will be sure to use the unfortunate scene in the final cut."

Ad swallowed dryly. "I see your point, Jett, but I can't help you."

Her lips turned to a mad dog snarl. A fingernail snagged the pocket of his jeans and tore. She exploded in a fusillade of expletives.

"Nothing personal, sweet cheeks, but I've got a job to do." He waved his arms expansively. "So do all these folks. We're on a budget, a time constraint, and my future as an assistant director is on the line here if we don't wrap this thing by the start of my next job." He shrugged. "So you see, I have no choice. Oh, and we're ready for you on the set."

The words strangled in her throat then squeaked out. "Are you nuts? I barely know my lines, my makeup's a mess, and now I have a broken nail. How could I possibly go on?"

"Wing it, sweet cheeks," he said, taking position near the camera. "You always have before."

"You'll never lay eyes on these 'sweet cheeks' again, you Neanderthal."

She rolled her mouth to form a particularly liquid spit wad to drop on his shoe but gave it up for the sake of her carefully applied lipstick. No sense in destroying all her dignity by a smudged lip line that was otherwise perfect. He wasn't worth it. Well, maybe he was. But pity the next person who crossed her today. They'd live to regret it, that's for sure.

Jett inhaled deeply, pulled herself up to full size while assuming an air of piety, then assumed her place on the set loveseat while glancing around to make sure there were no apparent renegade electrical cords.

Gig appeared from the dark of an inactive set, sat in her fire-engine red director's chair, and nodded.

A siren sounded.

Ad held the walkie-talkie close to his mouth. "Quiet, please. We're rolling."

"Speed."

A man in coveralls stood in front of the camera with the clapboard. "Scene twenty-two, take one."

Gig leaned forward in her chair, fingers crossed. "And action."

Jett picked up a TV remote and clicked it at a non-existent TV off stage. She clicked again. A bored look crossed her face. Sighing, she glanced covertly over her shoulder toward the living room front door and sighed louder.

She rolled her eyes and announced in angry tones, "There's *nothing* on *TV* in case *anyone* wants to *know*."

Beluga Stein's voice boomed from behind the door. "Now? Do I come out now?"

Gig leaped to her feet. "Cut. Ad, remind Ms. Stein that her cue is Jett's sigh, and 'Do I come out now?' is not a line from the script." She shook her head, eased back into the chair, and said to no one in particular, "I could've been a travel agent, but no. I had to be a low-budget film director. From the top, please."

Beluga's muted voice came from behind the set. "I forgot to push the doorbell, didn't I? Gig? Gig?"

"Yes, Ms. Stein."

"I'll get it this time."

"I'm sure you will. Are you ready now?

"Ready and willing."

"I'm glad to hear it, Ms. Stein. From the top, guys."

"Damn amateurs," Jett said under her breath.

"Scene twenty-two, take two."

"Speed."

"And action, please," Gig said.

Jett started over with the remote to the phantom TV and sighed like a disagreeable grizzly bear. A doorbell rang.

"It's open," she said in a sing-song voice.

The doorknob rattled and rocked in its frame, then turned. Beluga launched herself into the room. Planchette followed hot on her heels.

"That damned cat!" Jett shrieked.

Beluga snorted. "I believe the film you're referring to

was *That Darned Cat*. Planchette thought it was a bit on the clichéd side, but otherwise fairly entertaining."

"Cut." Gig rubbed her temples and said in a weary but commanding tone, "People, people, people. We have a picture to make. Jett, ignore the cat. Ms. Stein, please stick to the script. From the top. *Again*."

"Scene twenty-two, take three."

"Rolling."

"Speed."

"And, in case anyone gives a shit, action."

The remote. The TV. The doorbell.

"It's open," barked Jett.

Beluga twisted the doorknob and propelled her ample body into the room. "My nephew says you dumped him. How dare you!"

Jett rose, skirted a stray electrical wire, stepped over Planchette, who was sharpening his claws on the Persian rug, and reached into a desk drawer. "That's right. I did."

Assuming a look of severe stomach cramps, Beluga said, "But why? He's the kindest, most gentle of... you know."

"Bees. Say it. He's a *bee*." And here's the proof. Jett held up a jar filled with dark, viscous fluid. "Sourwood honey."

"That was always his favorite."

"Some people get engagement rings. I get...this."

"What's your point?"

Jett's face turned incredulous, then relaxed to boredom. "The relationship is off. There's nothing you can do."

Beluga stepped toward Jett, crossed her mark, and shuffled back a bit to meet it. "Oh, but there is."

"What are you? Some kind of queen bee?"

Eyes widening in her most menacing manner, Beluga nodded, smoothed back the hair on her forehead to reveal two small, manicured antennae, and smiled.

"Cut. Print it. We'll voice over Jett's reaction scream in editing. Set up the next shot." Gig whispered something to the cinematographer then drifted over to the two women. "Jett, you're up in the next scene. You may want to try an industrial strength adhesive on those fake eyelashes next time. One's stuck to your cheek."

Jett's hand went to her naked eye and then found the eyelash where Gig said it was. She pried it loose and wailed, "We have to do it again. Everyone come back. Turn those lights back on." She turned on the set designer. "Move that couch another foot, and you'll lose your life. Come back here, you little cretin."

"Get over it, Jett," Gig said. "The shot didn't pick it up. And," she glanced at her watch, "you've got about twenty minutes to make your repairs before you're up again. Better get cracking. Time's wasting."

Almost to the point of seizures, Jett whirled around for a viable, weak victim. Finding none, she yelled for Ad, who ducked into the film office without so much as a nod to her agonizing pain. The Neanderthal.

Who? Who would be the one to succumb to her wrath? Someone… Yes. Perfect.

"It's your fault, you…you amateur," she said to Beluga with a wicked witch sneer. "And your little cat, too." She stalked off and kicked out at Planchette, who sidestepped her just in time.

Beluga raised her hand and waggled it like a school child with an extremely important question. "So?"

"So, what, Ms. Stein?" asked Gig.

"Beluga."

"Of course. Beluga."

"So? How was I? Brilliant, or simply wonderful?"

"Not bad."

"Not bad?" Beluga scratched the antennae at her forehead. "That's it? Not bad? I'm so disappointed."

"Sorry, Beluga. I'm not one for praising. A job's a job. Yours, at least briefly, was to play the part of the bee aunt."

"The great-aunt. Although I'm not near old enough for the role, I found it a personal challenge. The operative word being 'great' in great-aunt."

"Whatever works. Listen, I have to get back to work. And from what I understand, so do you."

Beluga grinned hopefully. "Another scene?"

"No. Not right now."

"Oh."

"The unfortunate events on this picture… How do the police figure in all this?"

"They have their investigation. I have mine."

Gig seemed to think about this a split second. "Okay. But keep it out of the way of filming."

"I'll do my best. And, Gig?"

"Yes, Beluga."

"Got a crowbar somewhere so I can pry these antennae off my head?"

Gig laughed. "Low-budget, cheesy films, huh? They're a breed of their own. Yeah. Try the honey wagon door at the far end. It was the Bee Man's spot. Hope that kind of thing doesn't bother you."

"I'll let you know, Gig."

"I'm sure you will, Beluga. Look. There's Ashbole over there come to pay us a visit. Hopefully, a brief one. Wow, he looks worse than I heard. He's waving at us."

The electric generators suddenly groaned to a halt, causing a brownout, then total blackness. A second passed, two, when across the set, carpentry supplies clattered to the floor amid animated conversation and selective heated words.

"Strange," Beluga said. "Another power failure."

Gig dismissed this statement with a wave of her hand. "Low-budget films mean low-budget equipment and shanty-like stages. Don't give it another thought."

Motors coughed and sputtered to life. Dim light finally grew to the brighter working level. The crew collectively shrugged, then returned to work.

"See?" Gig said. "Back to normal already, and Ashbole didn't even panic."

"Yoo-hoo, Boley," Beluga yelled. "You missed my scene. I was great."

Boley nodded and beckoned Gig.

"He's calling me," Gig said. "I hope that wasn't a wink with his good eye. See you later, Beluga."

"See you, Gig."

A thought came to her. It was a partial thought at this point, not yet fully formed but effective in a nagging sort of way. Something to do with electrical problems. Power failures. Something... It was all very strange indeed.

Beluga scratched around one connection of antenna to her forehead. The previous nagging thought shifted to personal concern that she would have one serious rash if she didn't get these bee tentacles off in a hurry.

As it was, the heat of the lights and the seemingly decades-old wait to shoot the scene could mean the antennae would be permanently affixed. Then what would she do?

Custom ordering all future hats might be the least of

her worries. This was a sobering speculation and a highly motivating one.

"To the honey wagon. You coming, Planchette?"

Chapter 8

Beluga walked at a brisk pace across the stage parking lot to where the honey wagon sat, carefully avoiding the occasional ice patch. It was cold out here. Damn cold. Even for a February in Atlanta. The skin around her antennae contracted and puckered and became even more disagreeable than when she stood under the hot lights of the set.

Sympathy bubbled up within her for the hard life a regular bee had to live. Especially if their accouterments were attached with anything comparable to the adhesive she had to endure. She was little more than a bee stand-in, but this antenna bit was driving her to the very brink of insanity.

"Pick up the pace, Planchette. Shaking your feet at every step only prolongs the agony."

The cat yowled in misery.

"Give it up, or you wear the reindeer horns during the holiday season this time instead of Emerson."

Planchette stopped to lick a paw, glared at her, then grudgingly kept moving.

"That's my boy."

A slick spot caught her off guard and dropped her hard on her rump. She bumped, bounced, then slid uncontrollably toward a parked, pumpkin-orange disaster of a car. The collision was inevitable, undoubtedly would be tragic, and was, in a strange twist of fate, karmic. She had owned just such a model a very long time ago and didn't have good luck with that one either. At this very moment damage control was her only immediate hope. Rolling to one side, she bumped her head, knocked off one antenna, and crashed to a stop next to the car's back wheel.

Beluga lay there, still and cautious, waiting for some message from her neurons that there was a broken bone or impending exquisite pain. The all-clear sounded in her mind. She reached up to touch the empty spot on her forehead and sighed deeply as Planchette appeared at her side. "The good news is one antenna has been officially removed. The bad news is that I now look like a deranged unicorn."

Planchette nuzzled her face.

"Thanks for the sympathy, my dear feline, but if you don't mind, I think I'll just lie here a moment. Or until my undergarments start to freeze." She groaned and started to rise when she saw it. "What's this?"

Leaning toward the tire that stopped her body from hurtling at the speed of light through a neighboring industrial park, Beluga narrowed her eyes and stared. She reached out to scrape the residue on the tire then examined the results stuck to her fingernail. Latex. The stuff of antennae.

The stuff of the Bee Man's suit.

What was it doing on the original tires of this old, very old, disaster of a car? Original tires?

That was some dedicated vintage car owner. Or someone extraordinarily cheap. Or broke.

Beluga scraped more of the latex into her open palm and deposited it deep into the pocket of her costume housedress.

"Ms. Stein! Are you all right?" The kid production assistant ran to her and skittered across a patch of ice. Falling to his knees, he continued his slide, arms open, until he stopped beside her like an Olympic skater completing his routine to rousing applause.

"Careful. The pavement is icy."

"Yes, ma'am. You're right, and I think the knees to my blue jeans are gone."

"I could offer you a spare antenna."

"I think I passed it about six feet back."

Beluga laughed. "The one wedged to my scalp is all yours if you can figure out how to pry it off. That's what started this descent into frozen hell, to begin with."

The kid danced his way upright as if he had three times the normal number of joints, then stared at the gaping holes in his jeans.

"Nice knees."

"They've always worked for me."

"You're funny, kid. Now help me up. Careful now. There." Beluga stood with her feet far apart and took a tentative step.

"Something wrong with your back, Ms. Stein?"

"Contrary to the sumo-wrestler look, I'm trying to lower my center of gravity."

Another step, then a third. "Of course, on ice all bets are off. Still, it seemed worth a try." She paused in her great oak stance and looked at the honey wagon. "There are five doors on that trailer. Which one was the Bee Man's?"

"The one at the far end."

"Of course. It had to be the furthest away from here."

"It's the one next to Jett Blacke's."

"The one with the crescent moon carved on the

door?"

"Yup." He snickered. "That's the one. There was a moon on her motor home, too, but it was hauled away after the Jaws of Life kinda tore it up to get her out."

"I like it. I've seen a few real moon buildings where I live. The North Georgia mountains, in case you're interested. Used one or two crescent models, in fact, but I'm not particularly fond of the experience. Research, you know."

"I guess." The kid shrugged. "Can I assist you to the trailer?"

"That would be lovely."

"That's what I'm here for. Prod Ass, that's me," he said proudly. "That's short for production assistant."

"How vivid."

Beluga took the kid's arm. Together they slithered across the parking lot to the steps that led up to the Bee Man's trailer door.

"We're here, Ms. Stein. Be careful up those steps. I'll wait for you out here."

"You most certainly will not. It's cold as a witch's, uh, bosom, out here."

"Honest?" The PA allowed a hopeful smile, then a full grin at her nod. "Wow. No one else has ever let me go in."

"Child, trust me when I say I'm not like anyone else."

"Yes, ma'am." He jumped to the second step, opened the door, and went in. Leaning out, he offered words of caution. "You have to open the door halfway up the steps, or it doesn't work right. It's pretty tight in here."

"I'll take you at your word. Planchette, to the trailer. C'mon, boy. It's got to be warmer than out here. Good boy. That's right. Now, then." Beluga hoisted herself up the steps, closed the door then found her nose inches from the kid's Adam's apple. "You weren't kidding about the spacious accommodations, were you?"

"I'll sit on the corner of the bed. Maybe that'll help."

"Maybe. Why do I suddenly feel like a pimento jammed into an acutely small olive?"

"Ouch. I think I sat on something bad." The kid wriggled on the narrow bed, then reached under his rump. His eyes widened. "Wow. That's the biggest pair of scissors I've ever seen." Like a magician or a master of psychokinesis, he reached behind his prone body to produce a jumbo-sized container of paste and a handful of crumpled magazine pictures.

Beluga gasped, then twisted around in the narrow space for a better view. "Can you manifest anything else? You know, jewels, gold, or tickets to see the Chippendales?"

The kid grimaced, turned to one side, and groaned as he produced an open ream of white photocopy paper.

"Interesting," Beluga said. "It appears the Bee Man took an interest in decoupage."

"Or maybe he just liked to cut out pictures and glue them all together to make a new picture."

"Couldn't have said it better myself." Beluga scratched at the base of the remaining antenna and considered this new twist. "I've seen the results of this fascinating hobby. In my refrigerator, to be precise."

The kid cocked his head to one side. "Why? Does the cold air make a difference?"

"Not to my knowledge. Not that anything was cold anymore, mind you. The refrigerator has long since died."

The cat released a particularly plaintive yowl.

"Planchette still has nightmares about that ugly event. Don't you, boy?" Beluga reached down to pet him but was confined by the tight space that threatened to cut off all blood flow to her lower body if she chanced it. She opted to wink at the cat instead.

He winked back, then eased himself under the tiny desk wedged between the bed, the back wall, and the side wall that separated the Bee Man's room from Jett Blacke's.

The neighboring door in question slammed shut, causing the trailer to shake and the Bee Man's door to rattle in its thin frame.

Jett Blacke's muted but amply piercing voice traveled to them more in a series of physically felt tremors than actual coherent speech.

"Uh-oh." The kid scooted to the foot of the bed and writhed around Beluga's body. "She's calling me."

"How can you tell? An earthquake has diction better than that."

His eyes bulged like a bas-relief sculpture. "I can tell."

The two of them turned, twisted, and slid around each other like competitors in a greased pig competition until the kid found himself by the door.

"Listen," he said, backing out the door. "Sorry I couldn't help you with the antenna, but there's bound to be something in one of those drawers that'll work."

"Ah, antenna removal. My new life's work."

Jett Blacke's door flew open to slam against the side of the trailer. "Where the hell is the prod ass? Oh, there you are, you little weasel. Didn't you hear me call?"

"I'm sorry, Miss Blacke."

"That you are," she snarled.

Beluga wedged herself in the door frame. "Hello, Jett. Indulging yourself in another meditative moment?"

"Drop dead and die."

"A bit redundant, but I get your point. Say, Jett?" Beluga twisted at an oblique angle in the narrow door that threatened to shred a body part. "Did you ever hear anything going on in this room? The walls are a bit on the flimsy side."

"Flimsy?" The color under Jett's thick make-up paled a notch. "How flimsy?"

"Parchment. Drapery sheers." It was a blatant exaggeration, but she couldn't stop herself now. "Egg roll wrapper thin. Negligee transparent. Ad prefers the blood-red one, by the way. Mosquito net flimsy."

The production assistant snickered.

Jett turned on him with a malicious hiss. "Sit on it and spin."

"Yes, ma'am, Miss Blacke."

The trailer door slammed shut, followed by a scream that was abruptly discontinued.

Beluga shrugged. "At least we'll have a little quiet while the investigation continues."

She squirmed loose from the confining door and popped back into the room.

A minute passed.

Her head reappeared in the doorway. "Are you coming in or not?"

The kid shook his head. "I better not. I think I should wait here until I get further orders from Miss Blacke."

"I see," Beluga said. "Well, I always wondered what hell looks like when it's frozen."

"Ma'am?"

"Never mind. Still, I think it's safe to say that you

might have a little time on your hands."

"I don't think so."

True to his word, Jett's door banged open. "Coffee, no cream, six sugars. *Now*."

"Yes, ma'am, Miss Blacke."

"And bring me a bag of those cookies I like. A full, unopened, and unsullied by human hands bag, or your life is on the line. Oh, and a chocolate bar. With nuts." Jett sneered at Beluga. "Some of us don't have to watch our weight."

The door slammed shut.

"What a delightful creature she is," Beluga said. "You know, she's just what this country needs to fill the ranks of the diplomatic corps."

"Whatever." The kid skittered across the ice to complete his errands, then stopped. "The assistant director? A red negligee? That's rich."

"True, too," Beluga muttered under her breath. "Kid, before you leave me to my antenna surgery, tell me one thing."

"I'll try."

"Who owns the pumpkin-orange disaster of a car?"

"That's easy. I do."

"You?"

He puffed up with pride. "My parents gave it to me as a graduation present."

"They must love you very much," Beluga droned. "Has anyone working on the film ever borrowed it?"

"Yeah," he said. "Just about everyone. That's why I get to park in such a great place."

"I don't suppose you could make me a list of names, dates, and times when your car was borrowed."

"That'd be kinda hard, but I could try. I think Mr.

Ashbole keeps a list somewhere."

"I knew I could count on you. You're going to be a great filmmaker someday, kid."

"Honest?" He nodded, then grinned. "Yeah. That would be great. Really great."

Something that sounded like a fist slammed against the inside of Jett Blacke's door. The kid jumped straight into the air at the sound, turned one hundred and eighty degrees, then landed on his feet in a run to the stage building.

"There goes a very nice young man, Planchette. A bit on the timid side and, uh-oh, recovered now from a nasty fall, but with a slight limp. Still, all and all, he's a nice kid. His list will help narrow down the possible killers. At least, I hope it will." She turned to the cat grooming himself in preparation for a long nap. "At least we know he's not our killer. I can feel that much. In fact, I would bet the farm on it during a cutthroat tarot blackjack game. I'd even throw Emerson into the bet; that's how sure I am."

Planchette froze mid-groom and stared at her with hope in his eyes.

"Rhetorically speaking, of course. I could never bet my dear old bearded goat, and you know it."

Protest came by way of a tiny feline yowl.

"C'mon. You must miss Emerson just a little bit."

The yowl grew louder.

"Honestly, Planchette. Just because he thought you were a snack food is no reason to carry a grudge. It could happen to anyone. You have to move on. That said, the quicker we get our work done here, the quicker we'll get back home to Emerson."

Beluga sat on the bed to examine the magazine

scraps. "Part of the solution to the murder might be in the list our young man is compiling. And part may very well be in this pile of papers. But the most pressing issue of the moment remains painfully unresolved." She squinted at Planchette and pointed to her forehead. "How do I get this damn antenna off?"

Chapter 9

"Where is Beluga Stein?"

Beluga swept into the room. "You called, Boley. I came. Oh, ignore the small hemorrhage at my elbow." She pressed a wad of napkins to the scrape. "Seems my young escort is more sure-footed on ice than I am, being that he is only bruised from the neck down in his zeal to get us back to the building. I, on the other hand, as it were, may require minor surgery to reattach my lower arm after our fall." Beluga pulled a scarf out of one pocket and tied it around her wound with the useful hand and her teeth. "Gig, did you know our young man calls himself a 'Prod Ass?'"

"Oh, geez. Papers everywhere. And they had to be pictures cut out of magazines. Geez. A ghost did it. A *ghost*. Right?" Boley pleaded. "If you say it, I'll believe it."

"Of course you will."

The injury momentarily attended to, Beluga surveyed the room. It looked like the site of a propaganda bomb explosion.

"Hmm. Something happened. That's for sure." She dug into the cleavage of her costume housedress and pulled out a spatula to scratch at the remaining antenna stuck to her forehead.

Gig and Boley stared at her.

"What?" She stopped scratching and rolled her eyes

to the cooking utensil. "Oh, this. Fortunately for me, I ran into the caterers on the way to the office. Antonio the cook, and gorgeous, I hasten to add, provided my impromptu bandage. And the spatula. Suffice it to say there was no choice where I could transport it, and Antonio's life will never be the same. One hopes anyway."

"He's not bad," Gig said. "But he does have a wife and five kids."

Beluga winked. "Virility. I like that in a man."

Boley whined. The sound escalated to a shriek. "What about the ghost? That's what you're here for, remember?"

Beluga patted him on the shoulder with the spatula. "Now, let's not get our panties in a wad. I'm thinking."

He stomped his foot in what appeared to be the beginning of one of his legendary temper tantrums. "*Do* something."

Gig backed out the door. "This is where I take my leave."

"Hopefully not of your senses," Beluga added.

"Too late." Gig barked an order at the growing crowd outside the office and closed the door behind her.

"Now, then," Beluga said, taking a closer look around the room. "Talk about déjà vu; this is the clincher."

"I didn't do it."

"No one said you did, Boley."

"They all think I did it, but I didn't. Really."

"Aren't we being just a tad paranoid?"

"Just because they all think I did it doesn't make me paranoid."

"Boley, I believe I've read about this non-paranoia

paranoia in textbooks. You can do better than that."

"Perhaps he doth protest too much. That's what you're thinking, isn't it?"

"Why, Boley," Beluga said, examining a cut-out of a moth, "I didn't know you were familiar with Shakespeare."

"Honors English. I wanted to take Driver's Ed."

She reached for a picture of an old-time movie camera pasted on top of a fashion model that, if looked at in an oblique angle, could almost be Jett Blacke on a good day. A very good day. "So are you?"

"Am I what?"

"Protesting too much?"

He adopted the look of a deer caught in headlights. Clearing his throat, he then assumed an attorney-like intonation. "I don't have to answer that."

"Well, I suppose in a way you already have."

"I resent that."

"No, Boley. You resemble that. There's a marked difference." She pointed the spatula at him in an accusing manner. "Spill it."

He hesitated, found infinite interest in the toe of his scuffed loafer, then looked at her. "I don't want to, and you can't make me."

Breath escaped in a deep, frustrated sigh. "No, Boley, I can't make you. But by the same token, I can't seem to get the picture out of my mind of you in prison coveralls with a number over the breast pocket rather than, say, a polo pony or a duck."

"I cut out some magazine pictures."

"And…"

"Pasted them on white paper. Then I left them in the Bee Man's trailer. But he started it."

"The Bee Man?"

"He was trying to set me up."

"For his own murder? I don't think so." Beluga patted her pockets and peeked down her cleavage. "Oh, hell. I don't suppose you've got a cigarette on you?"

"Rat droppings and—"

"Carbon monoxide. Yes, I remember your Mumsy's insightful wisdom now." Beluga scratched the antenna with the spatula while stepping over the scattered papers and edged toward the desk to rummage through the drawers. "Continue. I'll frantically search for a smoke while you talk."

"The Bee Man wanted a bigger part in the movie and a producer credit. I wouldn't do it. That's when he said he'd hurt me and Jett. He was like that. Mean. Controlling. Then the magazine pictures appeared. Everywhere. I knew it was him."

"How?" She opened one drawer, then another. "Damn. I'll settle for a filterless about now. Go on."

"The supplies were ordered through the film company. I traced it back to him when I was reviewing the books. Actually, Father's accountant caught it, but that's another story."

The last drawer slammed shut.

"Not even a used wad of chewing tobacco. Honestly, what's wrong with you people?"

"Everyone thought the film was jinxed when the pictures started showing up in their duffel bags, purses, on the catering trays, in cars, even between the pages of scripts."

"Let's not forget my refrigerator." Beluga snorted.

A small smile settled on Boley's face. "I decided to fight fire with fire." The smile disappeared. "It almost worked, too."

"Until he was found dangling lifeless from a crane while trapped in a giant, latex bee costume sans one antenna."

"Yeah. Bummer." He touched his bruised, swollen eye and winced. "I didn't kill him. And I didn't put these papers all over the floor and desk."

Beluga shrugged. "Well, it's a sure bet the Bee Man didn't."

The phone rang. They both jumped.

"May I?" Beluga asked.

"Sure. Why not?"

She caught it mid-second ring. "Film office. How can I assist you?" A pause. "And *Guten Tag* to you, Tanya." Beluga covered the speaker with her hand and whispered to Boley, "German now. What's next? Urdu? Yes, Tanya, I'm still here. Yes, I'm thrilled that Luisa didn't have to wait long at the Frankfurt train station. Look, I'm a little busy now. What?" A longer pause. Beluga picked up a magazine cut-out on twenty-pound white paper, looked at it, and then carefully replaced it. "Apple strudel that cheap? Luisa is one lucky girl."

Beluga scratched the antenna, frowned, then glanced about the room at the display of papers about the desk and floor. Her eyes widened; her forehead wrinkled into deep crevasses. "Tanya? Tanya! Forget the recitation of Germany's transportation and food services for just a minute. Got your rune book handy? Yes, I'll wait." She nodded to Boley and pointed at the papers. "A pattern. See it? Not the papers themselves, but the negative image inside them. It looks like a symbol. Yes, Tanya. I'm here. What does the book say about *Teiwaz*? C'mon, Tanya, it's a rune included in the Germanic *futhark*. I think I know, but I want confirmation. Yes. Yes. Okay. I thought so. Good job, Tanya."

Another pause. Impatient, Beluga stared at the symbol and wriggled in place as if with a bad case of body hives. "I'll fill you in later. Yes. Right. My best to Luisa. Bye now." She dropped the phone into the cradle. "Talk your ear off; that's what she'll do. But she always comes through."

"I see it," Boley said. "It looks like an arrow."

"Good boy. *Teiwaz* is an ancient rune that indeed looks like an arrow."

A hollow, rumbling sound surged to life within the ceiling, rolled behind cheap plasterboard, then seemed to stop at the large vent on a side wall.

A high-pitched squeak produced a nominal air current that curled the edges of paper around the tip of the abstract arrow.

Beluga eyed the vent suspiciously. "It would seem that we were meant to look in that vent. I need nicotine." She lit, inhaled, then blew out smoke from an invisible cigarette and never blinked. "You open it."

Boley stepped back. "I'm not opening it.

"You're the producer."

"You're the psychic."

"Damn straight. And I don't like being a giant goose bump one bit." She took a deep drag on the non-existent cigarette then dropped it to the floor to grind under her heel. "As much as I hate to say it, we've got to open that vent."

"I'll get someone from the set construction crew," Boley said.

"Yeah, do that. But come back, or I'll hunt you down and kill you."

The door creaked open behind her. Boley's frantic footsteps echoed across the cement floor.

Planchette strolled in then stopped. Adopting his best electrocution pose, he growled from deep in the back of his throat, hissed, then flattened himself to slink under the desk. All that was visible now was the tip of his tail that twitched and danced as if at the discretion of a veteran, and imaginative, puppet master.

Boley returned breathless and with the entire available cast and crew. "I found someone."

Beluga surveyed the crowd. "What did you do? Make a bullhorn announcement?"

"Coming through," a female voice announced.

The crowd parted to admit a slight woman wearing a laden tool belt that seemed almost as big as she was. She positioned herself in the middle of the room.

"Geez, what a mess. So, you got a heating-air problem here?"

Beluga cocked her head toward the vent. "Remove it if you will."

"Sure. No problem." The woman reached around her back for an electric screwdriver, twirled it in her hand like a wild west gunfighter, pushed a button that sent the blade whirring, and approached the vent. "It'll just take a sec." Squatting in front of the vent, she attacked the first screw and revealed, through her now exposed lower back, just how heavy the tool belt was.

Boley gasped and stared appreciatively.

Beluga shook her head. "Now we know that tool belts and positive *derriere* cleavage tests are equal opportunity experiences. I always wondered about that."

One screw loosened and fell out, then a second.

"Almost there," the woman said.

The top of the metal vent groaned and bent partially open.

"I think there's something behind here." She peered into the dark. "Something big."

The collective audience of cast and crew gathered around the door rippled with under-breath mumblings and speculations.

"Could be a possum."

"Or a raccoon."

"I wouldn't want to be in a dark air vent and meet a raccoon that could bend metal like that."

"Oh. What? A lighted vent would make it better?"

"I don't do vents of any kind. Too creepy."

The woman shifted her tool belt and started on the remaining side screw. "That about does it."

Metal shrieked and folded under the dead weight that partially dropped out on the floor.

The room turned quiet as an empty tomb. Mouths opened in shocked silence, then recognition, and finally to total disbelief.

"It can't be," Beluga said to the stunned crowd while applying the spatula to her antenna.

Like a Greek chorus, they all said, "The Bee Man."

Beluga gasped. "I'll be damned. My antenna just popped off."

Beluga Stein's Diary

Ashes to ashes—for real this time—the Bee Man has become little more than a dust devil in the vent of time. Now there are even more pesky questions that remain unanswered.

Not to mention the distasteful, investigative authority-types who have converged on the soundstage to express profound unhappiness at the recent turn of events. It seems the Bee Man's apparent first death fueled mere dissatisfaction rather than the current unhappiness at a second appearance. For the investigators, it could have been a full-blown tick-off disguised as a mere miff for the little emotion they showed. They're good at attitude. Real good.

Needless to say, there is a definite lull in the party atmosphere. No lamp shades on the heads of cast and crew right now, that's for sure. And usually, there would be enough crime scene tape around the building that one might think we were changing the film to a thriller. They're more commercial, I've been told. And they get better distribution deals.

But thanks to Boley's esteemed father and his bribes, er, clout, we were spared the yellow tape.

Not so with the publicity. Every news service in the city has made this picture the top story. Tomorrow it'll be the downtown water main breaking and the ensuing sinkholes, but I'll let them make that discovery on their own. *The scandal-mongers need something to justify their colossal budget for coif lacquer guaranteed to hold every hair in place during hurricane-like winds.*

But I digress.

My inquiry for information from the ME's office produced a surly secretary who, in a fit of pique, dumped me into a fiber optic voice-mail hell that ultimately produced a platitude-spewing PR mouthpiece who took ten years off my life.

I remain undaunted. Mainly because I have a plan.

His name is Darwin.

Chapter 10

"Darwin!" Beluga said, capturing the young man in a bear hug that threatened to cut off his air supply. "So good of you to meet me here." Releasing him off-balance so that he fell into a high-backed booth in the crowded bar, she sat across from him, then motioned the waiter.

Darwin snarled in such a way that his meager black mustache moved across his upper lip like a sluggish inchworm. "It was a command performance, as I recall."

"Manned force?" she yelled over the din. "I don't follow you."

"Command… Oh, never mind." He smiled then, his eyes filled with admiration. "It's been a long time."

"I never forget a student. Especially one who works in the Medical Examiner's office."

"And I'll never forget your killer, cut-throat Comparative Anatomy of the Vertebrates class."

"You were my star student, Darwin."

"I barely passed."

"Bass? What have fish got to do with anything?" Beluga glanced at the throng of people pressed three-deep to the bar, all talking, it seemed, at once. "Is it loud in here to you?"

Darwin's face wrinkled in concern. "Shroud? What have you got yourself into now?"

The waiter approached. Beluga shouted in his ear, then waved Darwin to a more quiet part of the tavern.

They settled on a table under a mute television that would have benefited from a touch to the horizontal hold. The old cartoons playing on the screen rolled like they were on a ship in the midst of a tempest.

"There now," Beluga said, lighting a mauve cigarette. "Perhaps I can put together a coherent thought." She eyed Darwin suspiciously. "Good thing I ordered you a Bloody Mary and a burger all the way. It looks like you could use the calories."

"Yeah. Working weekends at the pathology lab and being a medical student doesn't leave a lot of time for eating. I splurge by watching the opening monologue on late-night shows, though. You gotta take a break now and then."

"The ME still working you like a dog?"

"More like a pack of dogs. We're underfunded, understaffed, and underpaid. The boss says it's good practice for when I get out of med school."

Beluga snorted. "The ME is a slave-driving old coot, and you can tell him I said so."

Darwin smiled. "I think you've made that perfectly clear all by yourself. Dad misses you, too, by the way. He never says anything, but I can tell. Your relationship together was as close to spice as he'll ever get."

"Thank you, dear. I consider that a compliment."

"I knew you would. It's just that he couldn't compete with Emerson being around all the time."

"Emerson is the love of my life."

"He's a goat, Beluga."

"One could say the same about your father."

The waiter placed a Bloody Mary and an Amaretto Sour in the middle of the table, then disappeared into the crowd.

"Emerson and your father have a lot in common, you know. Same hair coloring, beard, and, for that matter, disposition. Though, as far as I know, the ME doesn't attempt to eat hats and cans. Unless there's something you want to tell me."

"No hats and cans, but he's been known to spit a few nails now and then. Especially when he heard you called asking for confidential information."

"That's why I called you next, Darwin. The apple, in this case, has fallen from a different tree entirely."

"I figured as much."

The waiter slid a plate covered by a huge burger buried under a pile of red onions onto the table, followed by a basket of indecipherable food items fried dark brown. Next came a plate wielding a blob of unadorned tuna. Without a word, he vanished into a mob of office workers who had suddenly appeared.

Beluga pulled the tuna plate off the table to rest on the chair next to her pocket book and was met with a muted *yowl*. Darwin popped a potato wedge in his mouth, barely chewed, then swallowed it with a swig of Bloody Mary. "So, how is Planchette?"

"A little rattled after the body fell out of the vent. His appetite is off, so I'm trying to bribe him back to mental health. Tuna will usually do the trick." She stubbed out her cigarette and turned to the basket of dark brown fried stuff. "I really need to wrap this film, as it were, so Planchette and I can get back to Emerson and a normal life."

"As I recall, there was little love lost between your goat and cat."

"Well, there was that isolated incident when Emerson tried to eat Planchette, but I think they're working on a truce of sorts. Enough chit-chat. What have you discovered?"

Darwin hesitated. "I don't think there's a sling big enough to hold my butt if anyone finds out I told you this. Dad holds a pretty tight rein, you know."

"God, I miss that man and his rein."

Darwin winced. "Please. Can we stick to the topic at hand?"

"Don't worry; your information is safe. My lips are sealed."

"Since when?"

"Now, don't get all uppity on me, Darwin. Just because you're going to be a famous pathologist one of these days is no reason to be nasty to an old, er, former biology professor."

He laughed. "Some things never change, do they?"

"C'mon, tell all. You've practically inhaled your food, and I know you'll be out of here before I can wink."

"Okay." He looked around, then leaned in close. "Your second victim, the one you know as Bee Man Two, but is, in fact, the real Bee Man, was garroted. Official cause of death is listed as asphyxiation. The weapon might have been a wire of some sort."

"You mean like this?" Beluga plundered her purse. "Sorry, Planchette. This kind of wire?"

He took it from her and examined it. "Could be. Where did you get this?"

"Out of my antenna."

His eyes widened. "Your antenna?"

"Don't ask. It's a long story and a short piece. My antennae were small. Nubs really. One fell off in the parking lot. I pried the other loose with a spatula."

"A spatula."

"Correct. Inside the latex was this itty-bitty piece of wire. To make it flexible, one presumes, but durable."

Darwin stroked his mustache. "Latex, huh?"

"Pretty strange, but does it make any sense?"

"More than you know, Beluga. The first Bee Man victim, only known as 'John Doe,' right now, died of asphyxiation as well. Seems the air hole to his bee costume was plugged with hollow, tubular-shaped latex."

"Latex that might have held a long wire in it?"

"Yeah, maybe. But—"

"Don't interrupt me, Darwin. I'm on a roll. Latex, a long wire. Possibly used for an antenna. An antenna that broke off and was never replaced *on* the costume, but if parts of it were instead slipped *into* the costume... Then the victim is hoisted into the air where he can't get the head off, and presto, it's the flight of the mumble bee."

Darwin pointed at her. "We have the other antenna in the lab. The one that came with the body and the rest of the costume. I think I'll hone my dissection skills, take a little look into the inner workings of that antenna, then make an addendum or two to the records. The med school son of the ME scores a forensic point. Thanks, Beluga."

"My pleasure, Darwin. Oh, and here's something else." She poured a small pile of latex scrapings into his hand. "I got them off a tire parked on the stage lot. I bet these flakes will match the Bee Man's costume, but I defer to your office instrumentation."

"I'll see what I can do."

"But I'm still concerned about this 'John Doe.' Who is he?"

"That's why he's called 'John Doe,' Beluga. We don't know yet."

Beluga gathered her cat, purse, and the remains of the

tuna into a napkin. "Keep me posted, will you?"

"Ditto. Are you leaving? So soon? I've got another five minutes scheduled."

"Got to go. I've been invited to see the film dailies. Although under the circumstances, you might call them weeklies." She caught the confusion in Darwin's face. "Or maybe you wouldn't. It's a film thing."

"I'll call you."

Hoisting her bag over her shoulder, she waved and blew a kiss. "Toodle-oo, sweetie. My best to your father, the old coot. Tell him I'm keeping my bed warm just for him. The coffee table is another matter." She winked then stopped. "Don't tell him that last part, okay?"

"Trust me. I don't even want to think about it." Darwin shook his head and waved her away.

"Great. I'd like to keep it a surprise."

"Please, Beluga. That's my father you're talking about."

And it was. She could use a little male company again.

Not that Planchette, Emerson the goat, and her transient but imaginary, gorgeous male companion weren't enough most of the time.

"Oh, stop," she said to the illusory man while walking out the door. "I respect you. Always have. You're the man of my dreams. It's just that I get a little lonely now and then for the real thing. Even if he is an old coot who won't take my inquiries."

Chapter 11

Beluga squinted in the pitch-dark screening room while waving her arms frantically in front of her in an effort to find something solid. It was a moonless, midnight-dark in the small theatre with no overhead lights, running lights, and nary an usher with two rocks to beat together for a spark.

As dark as it was in here, even with technologically advanced surveillance equipment, her eyes would have a long way to go before she could obtain usable vision of any sort. Doubt crept into her mind. This was the place for the dailies, wasn't it?

"Anyone here?" she asked in a booming voice.

A chorus of "shhh" startled her into a back step that landed squarely on what she guessed was Planchette's tail.

The cat spewed a blood-curdling scream and launched himself like a rocket through the theatre.

She snapped her fingers for his attention, reached down to make amends, and cracked her skull solidly on the back of a seat. "Damn. I hate it when that happens. At least I can see stars now."

"Shhh."

"What on earth for?" Beluga asked, rubbing what was surely a permanent indentation across her forehead. "It's dark as a cave in here. Not one iota of light. That would indicate to me there is nothing to see. Therefore, I see no reason to hold back on disparaging comments."

"Be quiet."

This last utterance came from the direction of Beluga's left side. She turned to address the utterer.

"I assume you cannot see the disapproval on my face, which is a good thing since I am a lady of impeccable manners. Know, however, that the expression is there and it is not a pleasant one."

"Shhh," the crowd repeated.

"Have it your way. I could use the meditation time." She reached out blindly until her hand slammed the edge of an aisle seat. Moving slowly, she gauged the dimension of the seat and angled herself into someone's lap.

"This seat's taken," a female voice said.

"Pardon me." Beluga fondled the seat back across the aisle and fanned the air. "Anyone sitting here?" There was no response save a stray cough somewhere down front. "This is ridiculous."

She dug around in her purse and found a lighter. Flicking it, she was amazed to discover that the small flame produced an abundance of light and a large audience scattered about the theatre, all blinking as if they had received the gift of sight for the very first time. Settling into the nearest seat, she released the lighter's lever and plunged the group back into darkness.

Beluga sighed. She cleared her throat. The seat groaned under her shifting weight.

"Okay, I give up," she said. "What are we doing?"

Gig spoke then. "We're thinking, Beluga."

"Can't you do that with a functioning light fixture?"

"I suppose. But it might shed more light on the matter than we're prepared to deal with."

"I see," Beluga said. "No, on second thought, I don't

see a damn thing. That includes my hand in front of my face. C'mon, Gig. Give a concussion-ridden woman a break, or at least a hint."

"From the top, please," Gig yelled.

The screen flickered and came to life. The clapboard indicated the scene and take numbers.

Beluga leaned forward in her seat to watch.

The Bee Man flew high above the ground, single antenna bouncing in the wind. Soaring over the landscape, he looked down, nodded then tilted his body for the descent.

And there, way in the background, was the honey wagon, the parked orange disaster of a car, and a person in a costume.

"It's the Bee Man again!" Beluga shouted. "Wow, the magic of motion pictures. But what is he doing?"

"Shhh."

The flying Bee Man floated effortlessly toward the trailers and the car as if he were considering an appropriate landing site.

The grounded Bee Man, in full view now, turned the corner of the trailers and stood there in animated conversation with an unidentified male who appeared to have a single, bushy eyebrow that traversed his entire forehead. Their talk appeared to escalate into overt hand gestures, including one particularly rude one.

Beluga gasped. "Did you see that? How utterly distasteful but to the point, as it were."

"Quiet!"

On the ground, the Bee Man reached deep into his blue jeans pocket that lay just below the cumbersome latex thorax. A second later, he handed a thick envelope to the eyebrow man. The man flipped through the envelope, turned to leave, stopped, then raised a clenched fist.

The scene abruptly ended with what appeared to be visual static; then, the clapboard reappeared, indicating the start of the next scene.

The projector was shut off, and the theatre returned to its previous dark state.

A tinny voice from the projection room came on: "Once more with feeling?"

"I'll let you know," Gig said. "Well, Beluga. There it is."

"I wish I could share your cognitive insight, Gig. Frankly, I don't get it."

"Tell her, Rick."

The cameraman's seat squealed and creaked. "We had to cheat a bit, this being a low-budget movie and all. We shot the exterior, the outside scene, one day, developed it, then back-projected it onto a screen while we shot the Bee Man flying. This gives the impression of actual flight footage without the expense." He paused. "I don't know how we missed the background gaffe the first time around."

"Not that reshooting the exterior is a budget saver," Gig said. "The set-up time alone will set us even further back than I care to think about. Then there's the back-projection scene to do again." She moaned. "I don't want to think about it right now."

Rick jumped in again. "What Gig means is that it isn't kosher to have the Bee Man in flight at the same time he's walking around in the background shot."

"Kosher, I understand," Beluga said. "What exactly he was doing still escapes me. Any thoughts?"

"Making drug deals, maybe."

Beluga flicked her lighter in the direction of this last comment.

A woman with impressive cleavage bursting out of her low-cut shirt peered back at her through squinting eyelids. "I'm Betty, the film editor. Nice to meet you. I liked your work as the bee aunt. Jett Blacke could take a lesson."

"How nice of you to say so. Ouch." Beluga's lighter went out and then clicked to life again. "Drug deals? Please. Elaborate."

"It's just a theory. Don't hold me to it."

"I wouldn't dare. Just a sec. I think my thumb is on fire." The lighter died. Beluga blew on the flint and metal to cool it off, then flicked again. "You were saying."

"It was common knowledge," Betty said. "For a mind-altering time, call the Bee Man. He could get you just about anything. The deals supposedly went down by the craft services snack cart. And he could deal with the best of them."

"Hold that thought. My fingernail just melted and turned black."

The lighter winked out. Beluga scratched, nudged, and pounded the lighter into a resurrection, but it was no good.

"Gig, honey, while I appreciate the gravity of the moment, would you mind a little room illumination? I would hate to see the results of my lighter's revenge should it suddenly sputter to a last gasp."

"Lights, please," Gig ordered.

A dimmer switch brought the room from dusk to dawn to high noon in seconds.

"I thank you, and my remaining digits thank you." Beluga looked around the room. "Who are all these people?"

"Cast and crew mostly," Gig said. "A few friends and family thrown in. It seems this has become the best show in town. Under the bizarre circumstances and all."

"I see." Beluga squirmed in her seat to face the film editor and resume the questioning. "Sorry, by the way, for mistaking your, uh, endowments for a seat cushion awhile back."

"It's already forgotten." Betty leaned toward Beluga and flashed undulating cleavage that tried to execute an escape from the material binding it. "You can buy a pair just like these. Remind me, and I'll give you the name of the surgeon."

"Thanks, but I've grown fond of my originals." Beluga eyed the crowd, passively absorbing every detail of this conversation, save for a ripple of giggles and the occasional smirk covered by a hand. She shrugged, then mugged for the audience.

"It'll change your life. Trust me." The film editor winked.

Gig jumped to her feet and spoke with an edge in her voice. "Enough bosom banter for one day already. We have a film to make, and I don't know how in the hell we'll ever do it now."

"Is this drug thing true, Gig? It certainly offers one explanation for the amazing variety of delectables available on the craft services cart." Beluga grimaced. "Can there be any other excuse for marshmallow products like those orange peanut things? And, while I'm asking, who was the eyebrow with legs, and what was in the envelope he received?"

"The answer is 'I don't know' to any of your questions." Gig's voice grew an impatience Beluga had never heard before. "I don't have time for drugs or junk food, and I never laid eyes on this envelope thing before today."

"John Doe," Beluga said suddenly.

"Who?"

"He's our John Doe. I'll bet the film on it."

Gig rubbed her eyes and sighed. "You'd lose your bet. Primarily because this film is already in serious trouble. One delay after another does not bode well for completing a picture. That and losing half the crew to other jobs will do it every time."

"Don't forget the ghost," Rick added.

"Of course," Gig said, rolling her eyes. "How could I forget the ghost? Those who didn't have other jobs to go to claimed they did anyway. The grapevine tells us we have a crew of supernatural cowards with a streak of yellow down their backs as permanent as a bad tattoo and as wide as the interstate."

Rick nodded. "I lost my focus puller. The Best Boy is history, too."

"You still have me," the film editor announced in a sing-song voice. "I wouldn't leave for anything. This picture is going to be a cult classic." Betty glanced about at the cynical crowd. "It will. I'm never wrong. Never. Look, let me make a couple of phone calls, round up a few folks in need of last-minute work, and I'll pass the info on to Ad." She hesitated, pointed at her chest, then smiled at Beluga. "I'm telling you, these babies work like magic. In the editing room, professional meetings, and especially in the boudoir. Contacts are everything in this business, and I have the calling cards."

"Speaking of Ad," Beluga said, averting eye contact with the film editor and her assets, "where is our illustrious assistant director? Shouldn't he be here?"

Gig signaled the projection booth that the day was over. Lights began to wink out. "He's revamping the shooting schedule and calling in a few favors of his own. I only hope it works." She motioned the cast, crew, and spectators out of their seats. "Go home. Get some rest. You know where to reach me if any of you get a salvageable idea."

The audience filed out amid evening good-byes, see you laters, thanks for the show, and the one from Betty, the film editor, "It'll change your life. I guarantee it. Call me."

The director tapped Beluga on the shoulder. "Knowing how you feel about the dark, suppose we step outside under a streetlight and share a few words."

"I'd be delighted, Gig."

The two women walked out the door. Gig slammed it shut, locked it then nodded toward a nearby cement bench. A power-cut in the overhanging tree branches allowed a slit of yellow street lamplight to filter down to the bench where the women sat and assumed cadaver-like complexions.

"Whoa, honey," Beluga said, bouncing up like a jack-in-the-box. "Couldn't you have picked a block of ice to rest our rumps upon? It's bound to be warmer than this."

"Sit down, Beluga." Gig sighed and glanced away distractedly. "Let me see if I've got all this straight. Okay?"

"Shoot. And shoot me if I get permanently stuck to this bench. I don't want to be discovered like this."

"Electrical wires with a mind of their own, a fire, magazine cut-out notes, a film behind schedule, over-budget, and now missing most of the crew, unexplained accidents, talk of ghosts, and two dead bodies." She paused. "One of which is unknown. Does that pretty well sum it up?"

"You don't miss a thing, do you, Gig?"

"I miss more than you know. A sane way of making a living, for one. How about you?"

"I miss Emerson."

"Who?"

"My goat."

"Of course."

"And, of late, I find I miss human male companionship."

"As opposed to what?"

"My imaginary male friend."

"I had to ask." Gig shrugged. "Well, that's life in the pictures. Romance blooms between scenes, a few moments become memorable then it ends just about the time the film wraps. A fantasy. It's all one big fantasy; then you move on. Most of us anyway." She sighed. "Got a cigarette?"

"Gig, I'm surprised," Beluga said, digging around in her purse. "And utterly honored."

"Just hand one over and shut up about it. I'd almost eat one of those orange peanut things right about now, too. Almost. Thanks." Gig unzipped her fanny pack, dug through assorted small tools to pull out a lighter, and lit both their cigarettes. She took a deep drag then released the smoke in slow puffs.

"On a self-destructive mission, Gig?"

"Don't need one. The film is taking care of that just fine."

"You've got another job, too?"

"Yep. But I've also got a contract on this one.

Besides, it's a matter of pride to get this thing in the can. I don't give up easily, Beluga, but it's tempting to give up now. Real tempting."

"But you won't give up."

"No." Gig smoked in silence, then stubbed out her cigarette. "I know the eyebrow, man."

Beluga sputtered and coughed, reached for her throat in the universal choking sign, then raised her arms high above her head.

Gig whacked Beluga on the back. "Are you going to make it? By the way, lifting your arms like that doesn't do a thing."

Arms outstretched, Beluga lowered them in a bow then repeated the sequence twice more. "Praise Buddha," she said, through fits of new coughing. "This may be the breakthrough we need." Recovered, she whirled in place on the bench toward Gig, grimaced with the chill, then asked: "Who is he?"

"A DGA spy."

"I love this job. The intrigue, the suspense, the new terminology. What's a DGA?"

"The Director's Guild. The union sends spies out now and then to make sure the director is following all the rules."

"So? There's a problem?"

"Yeah, Beluga. I'm union, and this film isn't."

"Oops."

"That's an understatement if I ever heard one. I could be kicked out. All that hard work right down the tubes." Gig swallowed hard. "See, the thing is, Siler is from California, and here we are in a rundown warehouse in Georgia making a low-budget, nothing movie. Someone had to have squealed."

"Double oops."

"At least. I didn't know he was in town until I saw the dailies tonight. His film debut was a real show-stopper."

"As it were."

"As if we needed something else to bring a grinding halt to this picture."

"But, Gig, if he's the John Doe—"

"Then there's bound to be all kinds of stink coming from this particular pile of—"

"Point taken. Well, a simple eyebrow man inquiry of the ME's office will clarify a lot. You say his name is Siler?"

"Yeah. Sanders Siler."

"Let me write that down." Beluga reached into her purse. "Oops. I forgot about Planchette's leftover tuna." She stopped, then snapped the bag shut. "Planchette? Here boy. Planchette. Oh, no. I think he's locked in the screening room."

"C'mon, I'll let you in. I've got the key. Just about everyone on this film has one. I even keep a change of business clothes in there. You never know when an important meeting will pop up demanding the professional woman costume."

"Move it, honey," Beluga said, nudging Gig to a faster pace. "There's nothing worse than a cat scorned."

"Here we go. I think there's a light somewhere on the wall. There."

Beluga ran into the room. "Planchette, where are you, boy? I hope you're in here or I don't know what I'll do. Planchette!"

At first, it was the sound of claws being sharpened on a theatre seat. Next, it was a plaintive *yowl* that turned instantly to one of belligerence, followed by sullen silence.

"Show me your smug feline face, Planchette, or there'll be no more treats in your bowl for a week."

"That's kind of harsh, isn't it?" Gig asked.

"Planchette makes Emerson's goat stubbornness look like child's play." Beluga patted her thigh then snapped her fingers. "C'mon, Planchette. Let's go home. There you are, my sweet boy. What's this? He's got something stuck to his hindquarters."

"Looks like one of those sticky-backed notes."

"It is. Since when have you needed written reminders, Planchette? Hold on. There. Got it. Now stop carrying on. It only took a few hairs with it. You'll never miss them." Beluga looked at the handwriting on the note. "Interesting."

"What does it say?"

"I'm not sure. It's rather cryptic."

Gig snatched the note from Beluga's hand. "Let me see it." She examined the paper then rendered a verdict. "I know this address. And see this? It's tomorrow's date."

Beluga snatched the note back. "Get out of town! Or perhaps this is out of town. Well, well, well. Looks like stake-out time to me. I've always wanted to do that. For a legitimate reason anyway."

"Don't you think this may be something for the police?"

"Absolutely not, Gig. They've got their hands full with traffic tickets and other trivial matters."

"Like two murders?"

"Why muddy the waters? Besides, for all we know this could be a lunch date, a doctor's appointment, or a stop at a convenience store for a loaf of bread."

"Not that address."

"And I want to hear all about it. In the meantime, walk me to my car. I've got some planning to do before tomorrow's rendezvous with destiny."

Chapter 12

Ad sat at the dining room table with an eraser poised over yet another version of the shooting schedule. He deliberated, negotiated, argued, then decided. Rumpling the paper into a tight ball, he tossed it into the growing pile on the floor next to his boots and reached for a clean sheet.

"Ad, honey," Jett Blacke whined from down the hall, "I'm lonely."

"In a minute." He pulled the gooseneck lamp closer to the stack of papers, squinted in the glare, then took a deep swig from the beer bottle. The pencil point almost touched paper before she interrupted again, thus sending his last coherent thought into a mental storm.

Jett's voice became akin to the sound of fingernails on a chalkboard. "Adddd. I'm getting impatient. You know it's not fun when I get impatient."

"I'm busy. Okay?"

"And I'm wearing the red negligee you like so much." A pause. She giggled. "Hey, I know. We can play Crazed Bull again. I'll be the cape."

"I'm busy, Jett."

A longer pause. "I'm beginning to see red myself, Ad. It's not a pretty sight."

"I'll take my chances." He finished the beer, pushed the bottle toward the collection of empties at the end of the table, and got up for another one.

Her tone turned threatening. "Your loss, sweetie." Sounds of movement in the bedroom traveled down the hall. "I don't share my passion with just anyone, you know."

Just whoever happens to be available at the time.

"Use it or lose it."

She had certainly cultivated that adage.

"After all, I've done for you, and you can't spare fifteen lousy minutes for my needs."

Her needs were endless. A veritable bottomless pit of demanding and unfulfilled needs. He opened the refrigerator, grabbed the last beer, and took it back into the dining room.

"You are a thankless, pitiable lout, and I think I hate you."

Now there was some good news. Maybe she'd dump him before he had to expend the energy for the same result. Filming was coming to a close, either from real or the recent dire events. One way or the other, it was a matter of time. This particular movie romance had run its course, and he couldn't be happier about it.

"But since I'm practicing forgiveness, I'll let it go. This time. Don't try me again, Ad, or your miserable existence will be little more than a used piece of gum stuck to the shoe of life."

Now there was a real motivator for keeping the relationship. What did she take him for? A chump? He twisted the cap off the new bottle and downed half the contents in one swallow. Wiping his mouth with the back of his hand, he released a tenor belch and considered her "forgiveness" approach. It was a manipulation, pure and simple. Like everything else she said or did. And while at first he found her behavior funny, attractive even in a strange sort of way, now he could barely restrain himself from running into the street to stand in front of an out-of-control, on-coming semi fully loaded with frozen foods.

He would have to end this. The sooner, the better, and as pain-free as a bandage ripped quickly off a healing wound. Anything less and she would make him bleed.

"Did you hear me?"

In his mind's eye, Ad saw the familiar growing curl in her lip.

"I'm talking to you."

Jett's lip curl would be followed by the sneer and the baring of blinding-white capped teeth.

"Don't make me come out there," she threatened.

He twirled the pencil, then attempted to make a legitimate notation on the new schedule but found himself drawing fangs in the cast column instead. "I wouldn't dream of insisting upon any form of exertion on your part, Jett."

"Too late." She stood behind him. "I'm here, and I'm not happy."

He turned in his chair to look at her.

The red negligee had succumbed to baggy sweats. Her face, buried under a cracking, green cream, appeared to have holes cut from it for her narrowed eyes and pinched mouth.

"I see you've taken an interest in Kabuki," Ad said.

"And I see that you're a bigger moron than I realized."

"True enough. Kabuki has a white base." He scanned her bizarre ensemble. "Gloves again tonight?"

"My hands were a little on the dry side." Jett softened a notch. "Be a love and rub fresh lemon halves on my elbows."

"Jett, try to understand this. I'm the assistant director. With that title comes a lot of responsibility. One of which is scheduling the scenes to be shot and the actors needed in those shots. With the few remaining crew I have left, my job has suddenly become a lot tougher."

"The lemons will only take a minute."

"Forget it, Jett. You're on your own with the citrus fetish. I don't have a minute. That's why I didn't go to the dailies tonight."

Jett's mouth fell open in shock. "You didn't take the night off for me?"

"Of course not."

"Of course not? *Of course not?* Why you little—"

She swung her hand across the table. The gooseneck lamp caught on her arm, whirled three-hundred and sixty degrees, then slammed against the far wall spraying the floor with shards of light bulb glass. Grabbing a fistful of scheduling papers, she flung them into the air then kicked the pile of wadded paper balls into an avalanche. A final sweeping gesture toppled the collection of empty beer bottles like bowling pins.

She stopped then, breathed a sigh of relief, and offered a tight smile. "I feel a little better now, don't you?"

Ad stared at the mess, a grim expression settling on his face, and grabbed for the half-filled beer bottle that remained standing, lest she go after it. "Much."

"Good. I know you want to spend every waking moment with me; I just need to remind you of it now and then. So, that's settled." A wedge of green face cream split apart, then slid to her neck like an iceberg calving. She retrieved the piece, pressed it back to its original position, then turned to leave. "Oh, I almost forgot." Jett reached into her sweatpants pocket and pulled out a magazine cut-out on twenty-pound, white paper. "I believe this is yours."

"Where did you get that?"

"It doesn't matter, does it? Not really. There's more where this came from, and I suspect the police would be very interested in this—how would one say it?—evidence."

"It's not what you think, Jett."

"Oh, but it is. Trust me, I know." She tucked the paper back into her pocket. "Anyhoo, I further suspect this new twist has added another, more positive, dimension to our relationship. On my terms for a change." Jett swaggered back to him, kissed him on the top of the head, and left for the bedroom. "Ad?" she yelled. "Make sure my call isn't until late afternoon. You know I need my beauty rest."

Ad fondled the beer bottle, then pulled a blank schedule sheet in front of him. A wedge of green face cream slid from his head where she had kissed him and landed squarely on the page.

He smiled. He downed the rest of the beer.

And then he wrote in her name for a six a.m. call.

Chapter 13

Beluga turned off the ignition to the ancient car, listened as it coughed and wheezed to silence in the cold morning air, and caught a glance of Planchette sleeping in the back seat. "I think we're surveillance set. All necessary equipment at the ready, Tanya?"

"*Naturlich.* Of course." Tanya rummaged through the supplies at her feet.

"Cat treats?"

"*Ja.*"

"Coffee?"

"*Richtig.* Right."

"Donuts?"

"*Sechs.* Six of them. Two glazed for you, the rest, assorted jellies, and one Bavarian cream, for me."

"I'll fight you for the Bavarian cream."

"You'd lose."

"No need to make a *schwein* out of yourself."

Tanya's blood-red lips became tightly pursed. She glared at Beluga through dangerously long, fake eyelashes and pointed a broken, synthetic fingernail. "*Ich bin sehr hungrig* at this ungodly time of day. I broke a nail trying to pry your coffee out of this cardboard cup holder-torture device. I'm the one speaking German. Not you. So don't cross me."

Beluga peeled the plastic top from her coffee, sipped, then grimaced at the bitterness. "I think someone got out

110

of the wrong side of bed this morning."

"This someone never got into bed in the first place, thanks to you."

"We had to form a plan, Tanya. Now that you're out of the hospital. Every good spy knows there must be a plan. Pass the sugar, please. And once again, welcome back to the uninstitutionalized, contrary to those hideous hospital-issued slipper socks on your feet."

Tanya handed Beluga a stack of sugar packets and a plastic stir stick. "I'm good, and I've been known to spy now and then, but does it have to be this early in the morning? Even during my short stint at the hospital, I left specific orders not to be awakened until well after eleven, followed by a breakfast of coffee and a sidecar, as well as erotic yet tasteful bedroom heels. Not that they paid a split-second of attention to my wishes." Tanya glanced out at the morning glare with one of her own. "*Mein Gott*, couldn't we have started this surveillance at, say, noon?"

"We've been through this a thousand times. The plan, remember?" Tearing open the packets with her teeth, Beluga dumped sugar into the coffee, then swirled the cup as if allowing a fine wine breathing time. "I have the address, and I have the date. The author of the note was remiss in including a specific time. Although he, or she, was generous with the smiley faces dotting the i's."

"So?"

"So, we wait. And we watch. And when the doors open, I'll mosey in and ask a few pointed questions."

"How long will this take? If my eyes miss their cucumber hour, I start looking like a basset hound."

"Tanya, my sweet, with those lashes, a cucumber slice couldn't get within vision test distance of your eyes. I'll take a donut now."

"Here. Take them both. Servitude is not part of my resume. Especially at the crack of dawn."

"It's more like the crack of nine. And assuming this business, like most others, opens at nine, we'll be ready for them. A few careful questions, and maybe things will fall in place." Beluga paused for a moment, then cleared her throat of the lump that was forming there. "As soon as this is over, I can get home to my dear goat, Emerson, and the mundane routine of teaching biology to undergraduates who'd much prefer practicing the concepts in backseats rather than a lab. I'm beginning to miss the quiet life of the living. Camera angles, back-screen projection, and latex costumes are a fun diversion, but the deaths of human souls are beginning to take a toll on me."

"It'll be okay. You'll see. I wouldn't trust solving this puzzle to anyone else but you. You're the most caring, dedicated person I know." Tanya sucked the jelly out of one donut and peered through the car window. "This is not what I'd call the better part of town."

"It's an industrial park in the suburbs. How dangerous can it be?"

"Anything outside Atlanta's perimeter is suspect if you ask me. Too much lawn, rabid wildlife, and suburban assault vehicles driven by soccer mothers sporting ponytails."

Beluga smiled at the easy banter she and her friend actively pursued and willingly jumped back into the game. "We're parked in a paved lot. And the only wildlife anywhere close is curled up in the backseat. Besides, Planchette's well on the way to being domesticated. Just ask him."

Tanya shuddered. "Look at that place. They can't

even do entrance doors right. What is that? A giant garage?"

"Special effects companies seem to prefer a unique environment. Pristine work stations, low pile carpeting, and Monet prints scattered about on white wallboard are, well, not conducive to the creative process."

"How do you know?"

"A guess. Besides, they work with chemicals and plastics that are best kept very, very far away from shag rugs. Look!" Beluga shifted behind the wheel, then cursed under her breath when hot coffee splashed into her lap. "The garage door is opening. It appears as if the work day has started."

"I haven't even finished my Bavarian cream," Tanya whined.

"Enjoy. I think I can handle this myself right now anyway. Besides, it's best to have someone at the ready in case we have to make a quick getaway." Beluga climbed out of the car and slammed the door.

"I wouldn't be caught dead driving this weak excuse for transportation."

Beluga leaned into the window. "Are you this surly naturally, or has it been your life's work?"

Tanya snarled and then sucked loudly on the Bavarian cream. "It's a gift. And it's dawn. Can I have your donut?"

"Knock yourself out. I mean that literally, by the way." Beluga opened the back door and roused the sleeping Planchette. "C'mon, boy. I'm counting on your superior achievement in detecting suspicious activity. There you go. Be back soon, Tanya."

Those last words fell on deaf ears as the windows to the car had already been systematically rolled up against the crisp morning air. Beluga ambled to the open garage door of the Special Effects offices, then glanced over her shoulder at her friend digging through the donut bag while disappearing behind a growing film of window condensation.

"You gotta love her." She smiled, blew a kiss that Tanya never saw, then took a deep breath in preparation for discovering what she was looking for.

Whatever that was. Maybe she'd know it when she saw it.

Crossing the threshold of the open garage door, she raised her hand in greeting.

A child-sized latex parrot covered in synthetic boa feathers and clenching a beer can in one of its talons, dropped from overhead and shrieked at her. "What are doing here? What do you want?" The words were spoken around an overly large marijuana cigarette clone that was embedded solidly within the bird's shiny white teeth.

She leapt back. "Ganesha on a bicycle!"

The parrot looked at her suspiciously, cocked his head from side to side, then replied: "He's not here right now. Will Gandhi do?" Its lower jaw dropped open, and it cackled long and loud. "Good one, huh?"

Beluga stared at this deranged puppet-thing, then looked around the warehouse for a sign of human habitation.

"What's the matter?" the bird heckled. "I'm not good enough for you?"

"Oh, shut up, you reject." She swatted at the parrot, but it swung out of reach, then pelted her with droppings. "What the hell is—all right. All right. I'll play. Take me to your leader."

The parrot seemed to consider this for a moment.

"What's the magic word?"

"Please. Thank you. May I?"

"Wrong." The bird's lips peeled back in an ominous grin. Shiny white teeth glistened in the light. "Hitchcock Rules. Get it? *The Birds*?" The parrot swung back and forth, cackled uproariously, and then took a deep swig from the beer can. After wiping its beak with the back of a wing, it cocked his head to a closed door off to one side. "In there. We've been expecting you." The bird winked, then shot up to the ceiling and into a plywood box that slammed shut.

Beluga dry swallowed and wiped beads of perspiration off her forehead. This place was a madhouse. A complete, total, deranged, certifiable madhouse.

The side door opened with a creak followed by a drawn-out groan. A long-fingered, cadaverous-looking hand flipped down from the frame and beckoned her in.

She stopped, looked back at the waiting car with its windows totally fogged up, and considered bolting. No case, however intriguing, was worth this voluntary dementia.

Inviting male laughter burst from the open door and the room beyond.

On the other hand, things could get rather interesting.

A single deep voice punctuated the din. "Beautiful, Gore-Man. Can you make the eyes bulge a little more? Good. That's it. Now, turn on the saliva. All right!"

Beluga knocked on the doorframe a safe distance away from the beckoning hand. "Excuse me?"

A man with a beer gut and a goatee waved her into a seat next to a skeleton wearing a beret. "Come in. We'll be with you in a sec. Hit it, Gore-Man. This time with feeling."

Gore-Man, a slender boy no more than seventeen, tucked his fingers into a series of metal rings to manipulate the zombie head. Blood-red eyes ballooned out, its necrotic face smiled, then chattered the few remaining brown teeth. A copious rush of viscous liquid spewed from its gaped mouth, followed by a standing ovation and enthusiastic applause from the group watching this performance.

The goateed man slapped the teen on the back and wiped moisture from his eyes. "Beautiful," he said, his voice cracking. "I loved it. Keep up the good work." The group dispersed instantly and scattered to various workstations around the warehouse. "Nothing like a good jump-start to the day."

Gore-Man gathered up the zombie head and assorted instruments, then nodded to Beluga.

"Yes, that's her," Goatee said. "Leave this brilliant piece of technological zombie magic on my desk here, then go get what you need from the supply closet to do her."

Beluga's eyebrows shot up. "I beg your pardon."

"We keep a tight schedule here." The goateed man pulled her up by the arm, deposited her onto a stool, and slid off her coat in one practiced motion. "Good. You wore something you can throw away afterward. What is that? Some kind of bag lady dress?"

"It's a muumuu; thank you very much. One I'm keeping. And I'll ask you to keep your hands off it. And me."

"You're a live one, lady. But that caftan will never be the same after today."

"Pity the same can't be said about you. And the bizarre company you keep."

"Finest kind of company. Beats the walking dead who work desk jobs." He opened an industrial size container of petroleum jelly and gouged a small paintbrush into it. "There's my Gore-Man. She's all yours, kid."

Beluga cleared her throat in the most commanding way she could muster and stopped Goatee's exit. "I don't think I have a firm grasp of the situation here. Your name might be a nice ice breaker."

Goatee seemed startled. He smiled then and offered his hand. "Chuck Masters. I'm the owner of Magic and Madness Special Effects. You've already met Polly Want A Cracker, a big cracker. And Gore-Man here is young, but he's the best. Your head is in good hands."

"My head?" Beluga gasped. "What's my head got to do with anything?"

Chuck Masters laughed and patted her knee. "Just sit back, relax. It'll only take an hour or so. Besides, I think you'll find this a fun place to hang out." He prodded Gore-Man in the ribs. "Loved the zombie. Loved it. I can hardly wait for the corpse." He winked and left.

At that very moment, Beluga knew who the model was for the pathological parrot with the heckling voice. Undoubtedly somewhere in the building, someone manipulated the grotesque bird by slipping fingers into metal rings.

SFX people were a strange breed indeed.

Gore-Man scratched a pimple, then began work with the experience of an old veteran. After laying some kind of plaster material next to a bowl of warm water, he tucked dishtowels into the neck of Beluga's muumuu.

"Kind, young sir, I'm here to ask a few questions, and I'm sure plaster was not on my top ten list."

He shrugged, then pulled a skull cap over her hair.

"Ah, a talkative one. Why doesn't that surprise me?" Beluga scratched under the rim of the tight skull cap and pondered the residual effects of cutting off blood flow to one's scalp and face. "So, my dear mute one, does everyone get the benefit of a facial upon their first visit to this house of horrors?"

The kid grimaced, belched, then stroked petroleum jelly across her forehead with the paintbrush.

"Okay, enough all ready." Beluga grabbed the kid's hand in a tight grip. "I think you may have the wrong person. I'm not here to join your cast of the rubber dead. I'm here for information. Obviously, you have no proclivity in the use of language, and I need answers. So grease someone who doesn't have something better to do."

He stepped back and looked at her long and hard.

She glared defensively.

In the warehouse, the parrot dropped from its ceiling box and squawked. "Welcome to Birdland. Got anything to eat?"

Gorgeous Ad ducked the lethal parrot and entered the cavernous room. His boots tapped quickly across the cement floor. Clearly, he had been here before, but this time he didn't seem happy about it. "Masters," he shouted. "I need to talk to you. Pronto."

Now here was an interesting twist. Beluga considered calling out to the assistant director, then remembered her covert mission.

From her perch on the stool by the cadaveric-hand door, she could keep an eye out on Ad and anyone else that dared enter these harrowed halls. The parrot would alert her to their comings and goings, and the resonant warehouse would make her privy to their conversations.

Snooping didn't get much better than this.

Or much easier.

Rock music suddenly blared from speakers tucked around the building. An employee clad in blue jeans consisting of more holes than material kick-stepped across the floor while playing air guitar.

So much for easy aural eavesdropping. Still, there were visual clues available from this vantage point. That was something. And from the oddity of this place, probably lots to see. She looked at the teen named Gore-Man and decided that her mistaken head identity was karmic. And a great break.

"My apologies, young man. Proceed. I will cause you no further disturbance."

The look on his face clearly indicated suspicion. After a brief pause for what seemed intense deliberation, he continued painting her face with the greasy jelly "Close your eyes."

"He speaks! But I find your request—"

A brush grazed her eyes, and she closed them barely in time. "How can I possibly watch—" A brushstroke across her lips silenced the protest. She popped open one gooey eye in time to see Ad and Chuck Masters of Magic and Madness Special Effects, nose-to-nose in a disagreement.

Gore-Man jammed a straw into each of Beluga's nostrils. She sputtered and sneezed them out.

"If you're offering me a soda, young man, I fear for your knowledge of anatomy."

"Breathe through them," he said, reinserting the straws. He then turned his attention to mixing the plaster material.

Beluga drew air deeply through the straws sticking obscenely out of her nostrils and realized it wasn't enough to sustain life. Between anoxia and a skull-cap that was logarithmically reducing her hat size with every passing second, she worried what shell of her former self would emerge after this nightmare ended.

"Now make a scary face and hold it," Gore-Man demanded. "Good. Don't move."

Beluga assumed the best grimace her face could hold. This was a simple matter since Ad was stalking out of the SFX building. She moaned under her breath.

"*Don't move*. Hold that face and close your eyes."

Why not? There was nothing to see now, and she had missed any chance of hearing a juicy conversation thanks to the deafening rock music. Patience was a virtue, and although both characteristics were not her strong suit, they were being tried to the hilt right now. Still, a deal between her and this Gore-Man was a deal, and one never knew what other fascinating things might happen by simply sitting quietly behind a special effects mask.

She endured the cold, gummy stuff the kid applied to her face, head and neck, and thought about the synchronicity of the sticky note that led her here in the first place and the sticky position she was in now.

Was gorgeous Ad the killer? If so, why? The how of the murder was sadly determined by Darwin and others at the ME's office, but there were still many questions unresolved.

Ad certainly had unlimited access to the soundstage, and the schedules of all the cast and crew. His position was one that demanded a working knowledge of all the equipment. And the hateful Jett Blacke was a convenient diversion of suspicion from him, being such a deserving target herself. If disagreeable personalities were a crime, Jett would have been hanged by now.

But Ad as killer just didn't seem to work. He wasn't the murdering type. It didn't feel quite psychically right to think otherwise. Still, when you added two plus two, it usually came to four.

But then, her psychic ability was notorious for its hit or miss—mostly miss—attempts. Or perhaps these shortcomings seemed more obvious now that she was actively encouraging a fulminating case of claustrophobia.

Breathing life-sustaining air through straws that seemed to be shrinking to the size of coffee stirrers was not Beluga's idea of a good time. Trapped in a rubberized head-lock among total strangers who'd probably never notice if she displayed *rigor mortis* behind this mold made things seem suddenly worse than she could have ever imagined.

Potentially fascinating events occurring in this building or not.

"Now we wait until it gets hard," the kid said. "I'll be back when it's time to peel you."

A centuries-old statue in Florence should get this hard. A petrified tree should know hard like this. But never, ever should anyone experience the heart-pounding fear of hearing a seventeen-year-old announce he would be back to "peel you."

Worry greater then missing the conversation between Ad and Chuck Masters and the potential clue they might have leaked, and fear more from the idea that this mold would stick to her worse than the almost-permanent bee antennae, was her mother's haunting words when Beluga was a child: *Don't make a face like that. It might stick.*

Panic coursed through her body. Not for the

knowledge her face would forever hold this gruesome grimace should she survive, but that she would perish under this helmet of gooey material with the only relic of her life that of latex. Tutankhamen could carry off the permanent look, but that was a different circumstance and a very different time. She couldn't even hope for a bust of herself sitting in a dark corner of the college biology library the way things were going. And certainly not this particular rendering.

Beluga inhaled deeply through the coffee stirrers that for all intents had dwindled further to the diameter of toothpicks and tried to quell the urge to write a nasty letter to the Silly Putty people. Or to scream like a madwoman. Whatever came first. Then new sounds drew her attention.

Concurrently the rock music stopped, and the parrot began.

"Finally. We've been expecting you."

There was no verbal response, just the sound of high heels clicking across the cement floor as the stranger approached Beluga.

High heels?

At least it sounded like that, although it was hard to be sure when one listened through solidifying swamp ooze. If they were heels, they certainly stood out in this workplace of shredded jeans and outcast, chemical-spattered athletic shoes.

Sure enough, the sound was coming closer. Closer.

Beluga sat very still in the hopes the visitor would think she was one of the assorted mannequins. A little more fleshy than the skeleton donning a beret, but just as appropriate to this place.

There was a rustling of papers on the desk, then a

grunt undoubtedly at the salivating zombie.

Say something, anything.

The screech of another rock song filled the room. The high volume was sure to cause a tsunami in her ears' semicircular canals and render her incapable of rational thought. At the very least, it blotted out any chance of determining just who this visitor was.

Between the sensory deprivation helmet and the pound of an overzealous bass player sending rhythm ripples through the floor, Beluga found herself in a difficult situation. There was little point in counting on one of the effects guys to produce a latent description. Gore-Man had proved himself voluntarily communication-impaired. So it was up to her and the little physical ability she had left to gather the facts.

One option was left, and there was only one chance to make that option work.

She slid off the stool and, arms swinging in front of her, combed the air for a human body. A second step, and a wild helicopter swing of arms hoping to touch something warm and living. Her foot caught on the corner of a furniture piece. She staggered forward and caught herself. Where was the high-heeled person? Precious time was wasting.

Another step.

Another wild swing.

"*Oomph!*"

Bingo!

"Well, I've seen it all now," Tanya said. "That's one way to shut you up. Pity I never thought of it myself."

Beluga stopped, grunted, then pointed toward where she thought the desk was. Then she shrugged and motioned for Tanya to respond.

"A book. Two words, first word…."

Trying to shake her head, "no," Beluga could only twist her body back and forth.

"I got it," Tanya yelled. "*Wuthering Heights*. That was a great book, but what's it got to do with your head in a rubber vice? And what is that sticking out of the goop in the vicinity of your nose?"

It was hopeless. Positively hopeless.

Or was it?

She pantomimed her need for paper and a pen and listened for signs that Tanya responded. Rapid, hollow-sounding, distressed, deep-sea scuba breathing seemed to reverberate in the mask. Beluga could almost feel her brain cells dying. She waved for Tanya to hurry. If her friend wasn't quick, Beluga would turn to stone, or worse, the grunting, high-heeled visitor would be gone without a clue to who she was.

Tanya's voice gurgled through the hardening muck as she pressed a thick rectangular pad and pencil into Beluga's hands. "It was the only thing I could find to write on, and you don't want to know what's sitting on top of the eraser."

Beluga scribbled a note and thrust it out to show Tanya.

"I don't know who was just here, dear. Now don't get yourself all agitated. You'll break your head if you keep bouncing around like that."

Tanya led Beluga back to the stool. "Sit down. Relax. I'll scope out the place and see what I can find. But I'll tell you one thing, if that lascivious parrot attacks me again, I'm taking a blowtorch to him. We'll just see how talky he is when he's chargrilled."

Beluga shooed Tanya out of the room and

contemplated this new madness in her life. Any other time she would have enjoyed a good laugh over this chain of events and a few drinks. There was nothing she could find amusing or even hopeful in this current situation. She pocketed the rectangular notepad and the pencil, then waited for destiny.

It approached from behind in the form of the young Gore-Man, who announced he would cut a flap in the back of her head mold. Her body tensed as something nicked her neck and traveled to the base of her crown. She felt Gore-Man position himself in front of her.

"Be still," he ordered as he grasped the sides of the new flap and pulled.

Nothing happened at first, then slowly, very slowly, the mask inched free of the skull cap and pulled at the skin on her face.

Great, just great. First a reverse mohawk of a hairdo, and now she would face life without a face.

Painfully and slowly, the mask began to release its hold until it was finally freed with an unpleasant sucking sound. Beluga gasped and inhaled fresh air. Then managed to catch a towel thrown at her by the young man as he scurried off into the recesses of the warehouse with her face held out like a rare treasure. Perhaps it would see more than she had today.

Tanya arrived breathless and pale. "Do you have any idea what these crazed people do for a living? I feel like I've died and been doomed to spend eternity in a sick wax museum."

"Never mind that, Tanya. Did you see a woman in high heels anywhere?"

"Not a woman in the place. It's testosterone city around here. Ask me if I love it. Hey, your real face is back. A little greasy, but it's the face I've grown to know."

Beluga wiped the towel across her face, then turned to the desk. "Help me snoop."

"Now you're talking."

"Whoever was in here did something with this desk. Let's see if we can figure it out. Uh-oh." Beluga turned to the approaching steps. "It's Chuck Masters of Magic and Madness Special Effects. Do something. Divert him, Tanya."

"Diversion is my specialty." Tanya took a deep breath, formed the most alluring smile she could muster, and approached the SFX boss with an outstretched hand. He accepted it, glanced at her slipper socks, and led her away from the office.

Beluga rifled the top of the desk and found nothing except assorted, meaningless drawings and construction notes and the dripping zombie head that leered at her from its static position. With a quick glance to the warehouse, she tried the drawers. They were a cluttered, disorganized mess of more papers, stained with fake blood and other chemically synthesized bodily fluids that were best left untouched. Nothing. There was nothing newly left here by anyone or, by the looks of it, recently touched.

Then she spotted it. Jutting out at an angle under the zombie's latex neck was a triangular-shaped area without any of the head's copious oozing saliva. Something had been here. She peered closer. She sniffed. It was sweet, viscous.

The zombie head had spewed a thick sugar syrup, and a triangular thing placed underneath the head prevented the syrup from pooling on the desk in that one place.

So the unknown person had retrieved something from the desk while Beluga was incarcerated in the suffocating mold.

Funny, she hadn't remembered anything under the head when Gore-Man placed it on the corner of the desk.

The corner of Chuck Masters' desk.

Masters had made a point of directing Gore-Man to position the head just so on that desk.

That meant the boss was in on it, she decided with triumph. Frustration immediately replaced her moment of insight. Masters was in on what? She had nothing but speculation and fantasy thinking to create and answer this puzzle. A dead end.

"We'll be in touch," Tanya announced in a sing-song voice over the rock music din.

"I'm looking forward to it," Chuck Masters mouthed, then shook her hand again.

Tanya winked at Beluga and strolled out the garage door to the parked primordial car. She nodded at a young woman who entered the warehouse at that moment.

The parrot's perch, sans parrot, dropped from the ceiling and swung back and forth. The music stopped.

"Helloooo," the young woman said. "Anyone here? I hope it's not too late for my head mold appointment."

That was Beluga's cue for a quick exit. The faster, the better. She grabbed her coat, skirted the cadaverous hand on the door frame, and loped across the room.

"Do you work here?" the young woman asked.

"No, no. Just passing through." Beluga picked up her pace and scouted the warehouse for a sign of her cat. "Planchette. Time to go, boy. I mean now."

Planchette poked his head around the outside corner

127

of the warehouse garage door. A rubber parrot claw was clenched between his teeth. A large feather stuck to the top of his head like a rakish hat.

"Oh no, Planchette. Not the parrot."

"Hey, you!" bellowed Chuck Masters.

"Run, Planchette. Run as fast as you can. The door's open, and Tanya's got the engine gunned. *Run*."

Chapter 14

Her apartment was dark and growing darker in the afternoon light. Beluga never considered flipping a switch to illuminate the drab dwelling provided to her while she worked on the movie. Bright, artificial light was simply too blatant a contrast to the grim murders and her state of mind. The solutions to these deaths, and her plans to have settled this matter by now, were cloaked in darkness.

So should she be. Dark was scary and seemingly boundless. But inherent in the dark was a comfort as well. In the inky black of the very dark, there was no further fear of missteps. The bottomless pit had a bottom, after all. There was a stopping point and very clear boundaries. And there was comfort in knowing that the pain could get no worse.

The dark of the room matched her mood perfectly and hid the letters in deep shadow.

She smoothed the muumuu covered in specks of head mold material and placed a bowl of cat food in front of Planchette. "It's not parrot, but perhaps you've had enough poultry for one day."

Beluga forced a smile and failed. Even a small joke with her familiar seemed pointless now.

Not even Tanya's banter competition on the way home had cheered her up. The rapid getaway from the SFX warehouse was certainly fuel enough, what with Tanya's rendition of a movie car chase scene and the clichéd cinematic dialogue. But somehow, it all seemed forced into a game that had lost its appeal by redundancy. As Beluga got closer to her dull apartment, her senses and enthusiasm dulled as well.

It was all an act anyway. An easy, natural act, loads of fun now and then, but an act just the same. The heckling and one-liners kept her from dwelling on the hard facts of her life. The stand-up comedy routine hid her loneliness. Witticisms masked the knowledge that she was getting nowhere on this case in a big hurry; self-deprecation was the best approach to counteract the truth so that she didn't know what to do next. She was winging it, and anyone with half the wit of a rutabaga knew it, if they bothered to take a moment of thought.

Then just when the dark coaxed her to one more step, the pit proved it had a bottom after all. Arrival of the letters today confirmed her position solidly between a rock and a hard place.

Planchette licked his lips, stretched, and yowled for her to make a lap. She sat at the kitchen table, waited for him to get settled in the folds of muumuu material, then reached for the mail for a second, closer read.

The letters had arrived in a single brown envelope bearing the seal of the college in the North Georgia mountains where she taught.

The first, a folded note from the college, announced in firm tones that she was expected back from sabbatical in one week. Expressing disappointment that she had not contacted them as requested, the president had taken the liberty to schedule her for more than a full load. Adding insult to injury, he also made her the freshman advisor. Should she decide not to abide by this arrangement, he had added in cold business tones, her resignation would be accepted. He would await her immediate reply.

Beluga snorted. Always on the lookout for a way to get rid of her, this was the president's latest in a long run of weak trump cards.

"Look, Planchette. It's from the president of the college."

She waved the paper in front of the cat and was pleased he didn't disappoint her. Planchette hissed, spit, then shredded the page with a double swipe of his front feet.

"Couldn't have said it better myself, my dear feline." She dropped the ragged letter to the floor and stomped on it. "The old, anal-retentive fool. Never did get over that shrimp incident at the Board of Trustees' picnic. Just because you beat him to the buffet table is no reason to carry a grudge all these years."

She reached for the letter, brought it back to the table, and smoothed it out. "Was it my fault that Mrs. President took that moment to swoon head first into the salmon mousse? I don't think so. Nor did I have anything to do with the ensuing food fight between the Retirement Village Cloggers and the student debate team." Beluga stared grimly at the letter. "Still, maybe this time he's got me. I can't afford to lose my job."

Pushing the note to one side, she reviewed one of the other two letters forwarded to her. The page covered in magazine cut-outs revealed meticulous lettering spelling out the word "killer" on top of a pair of scissors cutting through film spilling from a reel. A jet soaring across the top of the picture was stopped short by a filled inkwell.

It didn't take a rocket scientist to figure out the picture referred to Jett Blacke in some way. But was she the killer?

This information was more than Beluga could ever hope for if it were true. The idea that Jett would do time without the aid of mascara, red negligees, and packages of cookies unsullied by human hands was worth a passing fantasy.

But the bigger question was how this artist knew where to send the picture. Beluga didn't recall telling anyone where she taught. And why this circuitous route when her local apartment was so easily accessible and known to everyone on the cast and crew? That included the sender of the first collage she discovered in her dying refrigerator. It was crude, for sure.

Crude. And this one was meticulously planned and executed. An artist in terrorist's trappings. A detail type.

Of course! This picture was done by someone else. The Bee Man wasn't a candidate due to his unfortunate circumstances, and right now, Ashbole wouldn't dare. There wasn't enough steak *tartare* in Europe to quell the swelling if he were sent back to jail.

It was someone new. Someone who wanted to be sure, but safe, in getting a message to her. It was also clear that this new messenger was fully aware of the magazine cut-out underground that permeated the set, and further, more than willing to get Jett Blacke in a kind of trouble everyone else could only dream of.

"Damn, damn, *damn*," Beluga muttered.

Why couldn't this collage clown just write a note in simple declarative sentences, spill the beans, and be done with it? Did everything have to be so secretive? And painful? She eyed the remaining letter. Ah, pain. It either kept you on your toes or knocked you flat on your butt. Sometimes the hurt was little more than a scratch or a bruised knee, but on occasion, it cut deep into the heart.

Reading the last letter again, Beluga brushed away moisture from her eyes and dabbed at her nose. Fight it. Don't let it happen. Crying won't accomplish anything but prove your heart is weak. Or at least that it's frustrated and vulnerable.

Planchette rubbed his face against her chin and purred. Then he began kneading her chest as if to get her heart feeling again.

She accepted his act of affection with an uncontrollable release of tears and held him tight. Her sobs escalated and poured out pent-up rage and fear. Distressed wails punctured the air and surrounded her with personal torment of time lost and the memory of past words used as weapons of anger.

There was anger that seemed to know no boundaries. There were words that had cut to the quick faster than the sharpest blade. These word weapons could bring strong men to their knees to beg for mercy, but they came all too easily to a mother and daughter in the heat of familial battle.

Regret forced an ache in her belly she hadn't felt in a long time and was replaced with a tenderness she had missed. Olivia was nothing if not a chip off her mother's block. Secretly Beluga couldn't be prouder of this accomplishment.

Her storm of emotions passed and settled on annoying hiccups and hope for reconciliation after far too long.

"Thanks, Planchette. I can always count on you."

He yowled approval and jumped to the floor. She sniffed, hiccuped, ran her hand through her hair and the residual casting material that clung there, then reached for the phone to dial the number.

It was picked up on the third ring. Beluga swallowed hard and wiped her hand across her dripping nose.

"Baby? Honey? It's Momma. No, it's not a phone solicitation for siding. It's me. Really. How are you, sweetie? It's been such a long time."

Damn, this sieve of a nose. She sniffed, wiped. "I want to hear all about it, Olivia, but I'd rather do it in person. Uh, huh. Uh, huh." Hiccup. Sniff. "Would you? It'd be great to see you, and this place isn't so bad if you like dumps. Tomorrow? Promise?"

Beluga patted a muumuu pocket for a tissue. Empty. "I can hardly wait. The directions are on the kitchen table because I left without them, as usual. What's that?"

Her nose was running open-spigot now. She patted the other pocket and felt something there. "Yes, dear. Emerson still likes his beer, but don't give him any. I'm cutting him off. Besides, I think he prefers the can over the contents anyway."

Beluga dug deep in her pocket for the elusive tissue. "Tomorrow then. Drive carefully." She hiccuped. "Of course. I'm sorry. I know you're a safe driver. And Olivia, honey?" She paused then and savored the words she hadn't spoken in two years. "I love you."

She hung up and leaned into the wall for the first full smile of the afternoon. It was a second chance she thought she'd never have. Maybe things would be okay after all.

The tarot cards had called it, even considering the missing cards so she wasn't working with a full deck. The runes announced a reconciliation was a possibility. Even the pendulum swung to the "yes" side when she asked if she'd see her only child again. But when Beluga gazed into her crystal ball, all she saw was a bereft mother who needed to get her teeth cleaned, and her upper lip waxed.

So much for round polished crystal.

More important was that Olivia came home, and tomorrow they would see each other. It would be a happy, happy day, and things would be right again.

Beluga teared up again. "Now I'm the silly old fool, Planchette. Bet you never thought you'd hear me say that. But then, I never thought I'd see my daughter again. Now, where is that damn tissue?" She gouged deep into her muumuu pocket and fished around. "What's this?"

It was a pencil. A bloodshot eyeball connected to the eraser by way of a spring coil. She reached further into her pocket and pulled out an envelope. Scrawled on the back was the note she wrote to Tanya inquiring who had just been in the special effects office. Tanya had given her a stuffed envelope to write that note instead of a notepad. This was the envelope that sat under the zombie head and dripped corn syrup on one triangular corner.

What could she do but open it? It was in her psychic investigator job description to check out stuffed envelopes that found their way into her pocket, wasn't it? Sure it was. She was pretty sure anyway.

She tore open the top and gasped. Cash. Great gobs of it back-to-back, an inch and a half thick. And there was a little sticky note that read: "We're even-steven now," followed by a smiley face.

A smiley face?

The chances were that this scribble and rudimentary illustration was rendered by a woman. Beluga knew of no men who would use the phrase "even-steven" and wear high-heels at the same time. Well, save one from a previous ghost-hunting mission.

And to make things more interesting, the same type of sticky note and smiley face was found in the screening room.

Well, well, well, well, well. The field of suspects was finally beginning to narrow.

Then the thought hit her.

Ad.

He was the one who had sent the magazine picture.

Sure. Had to be. It made perfect sense. Ad was a detail man; his job demanded that. Undoubtedly he knew about the magazine cut-outs floating around the set. Everyone else did. And if he was getting just a tad tired of the cloying, narcissistic, and demanding Jett Blacke—and who wasn't?—what better way of getting rid of her than setting her up as a murderess? Wasn't it Gig who said in her knowledgeable directorial way that when filming was over, so were the romances?

Well, well, well. First, a reconciliation with her daughter, then a possible breakthrough on the case.

She flipped a switch and brought illumination to the room. Beluga's dark mood was beginning to see the light again. And maybe even the upper rim of the bottomless pit.

"Planchette! To the lotus position. Or to a comfortable couch. Whichever is easier to get out of."

Planchette yawned and stretched one leg over his shoulder for a grooming session.

"The couch it is. I'm beginning to get a plan."

Chapter 15

Beluga stood in the shadow of the hot set where filming of a scene was just about complete and waited.

Her hair was clean and clear of the casting material as best she could figure, but more the pity for her shower drain, which now gurgled as if trying to swallow molasses. She'd even donned pristine clothing that had stayed that way until a visit to the craft services cart changed everything.

Smoothing chocolate-dipped marshmallow cookie crumbs off her fresh muumuu, she held her stomach as it growled in protest for something a little more sweet. Perhaps the cousin of the chocolate-dipped cookie, an artificial imitation banana-flavored cookie would do.

"And...cut," Gig shouted. "That's lunch. I'd give each of you an hour, but we don't have it. So take thirty minutes and don't spend it all in one place. Someone tell Jett she's up after we dine. That ought to give her enough time to add another layer of lacquer to her face." The director scanned the schedule and mumbled. "Anyone see the SFX guy today?"

"Not me," Beluga answered a little too loudly. She crossed quickly to the dining area.

Lighting tree spots winked out all over the set, and the dim working lights turned on. The cast and crew turned into a colony of overactive ants carrying out their assigned duties while trying to work in a meal at the same time.

A line formed just outside the soundstage door and in front of the catering trailer. It would have been dark as a tomb out, save for the festive multi-colored party lights. They ran the length of the catering vehicle and traversed the distance to the adjoining table, which bore a selection of salads and desserts. It was cold, too. Ice was already forming in the coleslaw, and the butterscotch pudding looked like it had seen a better life a few days ago when it still had movement.

Beluga wedged herself in line behind the young production assistant and grabbed a plastic tray. "What would you suggest as an entree, my dear Prod Ass. I use the term with the utmost respect, remember."

"Yes, ma'am," he replied. "I accept it with pride. Let's see..." He surveyed the menu written on a chalkboard that swung from metal loops over the head of Antonio, the cook. "The vegetable lasagna isn't bad; the mystery meat is."

"Enough said. And why, by the way, is this meal called 'lunch' when it is past eight o'clock in the evening?"

"The union says we gotta have meals after working a certain number of hours. Whatever time of day, it's always called lunch."

Beluga considered this a moment. "I see. But this isn't a union film."

"People still get hungry."

"Indeed. And rules are meant to be broken."

The kid shrugged. "I guess. Oh! I got something for you." He dropped the paper on her tray. "It's the official mileage log. I didn't know there was one, it being my car and all. I think they owe me some mileage money. Hope it helps."

She patted him on the shoulder, "Thanks, hon. I knew you'd come through." The list of orange car drivers slid into her pocket as she stepped up to the catering trailer window. "So, what's cooking, Antonio?"

"Beluga!" He winked. She winked back. He double-winked. "For you, anything."

"How about your firm Italian body on a bed of lettuce?"

Antonio laughed and waved a spatula at her. "You are a bad girl, Beluga. A bad, bad girl."

"Would that were true. I'll take the vegetable lasagna."

"I'll make it a double for my friend. Here you go. Any cooking implements to go with that? My spatula is a changed man and has never seemed happier." Antonio leered. "I got a garlic press that can do wonders in the right hands."

"I'm sure you do, but I'll pass on the tools right now. See? No antennae."

The cook leaned over the counter and whispered, "Forget the butterscotch pudding. For you, I have something special." He disappeared into the greasy depths of the catering wagon, then reappeared with a large bowl of spumoni. "I made it myself. Enjoy in good health."

"Thanks, Antonio. I will. That is if I don't freeze as hard as this ice cream before I get the chance to eat it."

She skipped the salad table and walked back into the building where long portable tables had been set up for the meal. Glancing over the heads of the crew inhaling their meals so as to leave time for a quick smoke or other recreational habit, she spotted Ad and took a seat next to him. "Good evening, gorgeous Ad."

He shoveled a huge chunk of mystery meat into his mouth, then nodded.

"Long day, huh?"

Another nod. He shifted in his seat away from her and impaled a pale carrot with his fork.

"Good eats tonight." Beluga scrutinized the vegetable lasagna and went directly for the spumoni. "A gift," she explained, pointing to the dessert. "From Antonio, the cook. A lovely man. Quite a talented cook and ice cream maker. Handsome, too. Like you. But not near as cunning."

Ad took a large swig of coffee and wiped his mouth. "It's been a long day, Beluga. A very long day. Make your point if you've got one."

"No point, really. Just idle chitchat."

"I have no patience for idle chitchat and less time." He jabbed the remains of the mystery meat and shoved it into his mouth.

"Mystery meat. I wonder where that delightful little term was coined." She was baiting him. Maybe if he got defensive, he would tell her what she needed to know. "I suppose, with a small stretch of the imagination, of course, and a bit of familiarity, one could refer to you with that same term."

"What term?"

"Mystery meat, of course."

Ad faced her. "If you're trying to get a rise out of me, it's working."

"Pity Jett Blacke can't do the same thing." Beluga scooped ice cream from the bowl. "Or so she says."

"Enough!" Ad slammed his fists on either side of his plate.

Dishes up and down the length of the table bounced.

Silence fell across the room. He forced a tight smile on all the onlookers and failed to wave them back to their meal.

His voice lowered to an ominous level. "What's on your mind, Beluga?"

"Have I shown you pictures of my goat, Emerson?" She flipped open a picture and was cheered when the onlookers turned instantly stone-bored and went back to their private conversations.

"That's not what this is about, is it?"

"No, Ad," she whispered. "It's not a picture of Emerson. But it's a picture just the same. Perhaps you've seen it before?" She waved the collage in front of him. "Go ahead. Take a look. I just got it today."

"That's not necessary."

"You sent it, didn't you, Ad?"

"I didn't say that."

"Okay, just for the sake of argument—ice cream? No?—let's say you know who the killer is, and you wanted to make sure I figured it out. I mean, it's my job, after all, such as it is. But I was a little slow in putting it all together, and you happened to have information that would help wrap this thing up. So you send me a picture." She picked at the ice cream and chewed thoughtfully. "You with me so far?"

He didn't answer.

"Good. Anyway, here I am. Here you are. And here is the newly arrived picture. Why don't you tell me what you know, and let's be done with it?"

"I didn't send the picture."

"Did you make it?"

Ad hesitated, then looked over his shoulder. "Maybe."

"But you didn't send it?"

"That's right."

"Who did then?"

An ear-piercing scream sounded in the distance and grew closer. The door to the soundstage exploded open, and Jett Blacke, missing one bunny slipper, threw herself into a throng of set construction people.

"Do something. They're trying to take me away."

Ad cocked his head at the crazed Jett. "She sent it."

Beluga stared in stunned silence, then regained herself. "Does Jett know who the killer is?"

The assistant director shrugged. "Who knows? I certainly don't."

Jett's lip curled into an ugly snarl. "Is everyone *deaf*? I said do something. They're after me."

Gig sighed deeply, dropped her napkin next to her untouched plate, then rose. "Who's after you, Jett, this time?"

A middle-aged man, and his humorless female companion wearing a police uniform, strolled into the room.

Pointing with an accusing but highly theatrical gesture at the strangers, Jett shrieked, "They're after me! They want to take me away! *Do something!*" Then just as theatrically, she slumped to the floor.

"How can we help you?" Gig asked the visitors.

"This is a private matter concerning Ms. Blacke," the middle-aged man said.

Jett bounced up with a string of expletives. "Tell her. Tell them all the vicious lies you just accused me of, you, you, animal!"

The man shrugged. "We are here to arrest Jett Blacke for the murders of Sanders Siler and Winchester Rainey, aka The Bee Man." He nodded to his female companion, who reached for her handcuffs and stepped toward Jett.

The cast and crew gasped and collectively backed away while eyeing Jett suspiciously.

"Winchester Rainey?" Beluga asked, aghast. "What kind of name is that?"

Gig paled. "Are you sure about this?"

"I have a warrant, ma'am," the man answered.

Jett leaped on an empty seat, scrambled for the table top, and stood up victoriously; clenched fists raised high in the air. "You won't take me alive," she bellowed.

The table groaned, then buckled and dropped Jett to the floor among a pile of dishes, flatware, and uneaten mystery meat. The policewoman slapped cuffs on her and pulled her gently out of the rubble.

The melodramatic Jett scowled around the room at her colleagues. Her usual cold, imperious affect was instantly replaced with the confusion of a domestic pet with severe indigestion. She whimpered, "Oh God. What am I going to do?" Then was led away.

Animated conversation, speculation, and gossip erupted in the room. Walkie-talkies surged to life as word spread about Jett's arrest.

Gig collapsed into a chair and rubbed her temples. "It's over. The movie is done. How can I possibly finish it?"

Beluga turned to Ad. "Did you have anything to do with this?"

Ad shook his head. "I wanted to get rid of her, I confess it. But not like this. Never like this."

"It couldn't happen to a nicer person," Beluga admitted. "But I can't help feel that they've got the wrong one, and I plan to do something about it."

"What can you do?" Ad asked.

"I don't know. Yet. Rest assured that Beluga scorned is not a pretty sight."

Boley Ash sauntered through the open door with Betty the film editor at his side. He inhaled deeply and puffed out his chest. "A long day of seeing dailies and I come back to an open door on a cold day? Don't you people know that heat costs money?" He slammed the door shut. "So, what's for dinner? I'm starved. And what happened to the tables?"

Betty, the walking chest enhancement commercial, quickly scanned about the room. "Something happened. I'm sure." Her expression indicated curiosity more than concern. "They found the murderer, didn't they? Oh, no. Was it one of us? Did they arrest her?"

Gig walked over to Ashbole and told him the whole story. One of Betty's hands shot to her mouth at the news; the other hand clung to her ample cleavage.

Boley gasped and sputtered. His knees weakened, and threatened to drop him. He leaned heavily against an upended collapsed table. Color drained from his face, then turned it dusky gray. "The flea poops have Jett Blacke?" Fear touched his face, followed by the beginnings of deep rage.

The working lights to the soundstage dimmed and winked out. Silence stilled the crowd. From the deep black of the room, only the single, angry voice of Boley Ash could be heard.

"Someone will pay. No one does this to Jett Blacke and gets away with it. Not if I have anything to say about it."

Beluga box-stepped in the lightless room. What was it about Boley and wiring problems? The timing couldn't have been worse.

Or maybe, just maybe, it couldn't have been better.

She considered this interesting twist to an evening of twists. "Love conquers all, doesn't it, Boley?"

The lights flickered on, then went out again.

"It's okay, Boley," Beluga said. "We'll find a way to free Jett. You'll see. A few phone calls, a little thought, and she'll be back with us again. Then you can tell her how you feel."

The darkness hung cloying in the room. No surge of electricity this time.

A thought formed in her mind. With a mental *thunk,* a piece fell snugly into the puzzle. It was a wild guess, really, a bizarre theory by anyone else's standards, but it was the only thing she had right now. And if it worked...

"It's not your fault, Boley. No one's blaming you." She paused, took a deep breath, held it, then spoke the thought aloud. "Tell Max it's okay. No one will hurt you or him. I promise."

The wait seemed endless.

Someone coughed. Another scuffed a shoe across the cement floor.

Then it happened. The lights came on one at a time throughout the building as if touched by a single human hand.

Or that of a ghost.

The crowd blinked in the bright light, then stared at one another as if wondering what just happened but were afraid to ask. Collectively they seemed to decide that answers were best left hidden, so turned their attention to cleaning up dinner dishes and returning to work.

Boley stared at Beluga, then slowly walked to the film office, where he closed the door behind him.

"Who's Max?" Betty asked. "I don't know anyone

named Max, and I make it a point to know everyone on this movie." Her ample bosom heaved when she got no answer. Her eyes narrowed. "I'll ask Boley. He'll tell me. If not, someone will spill it. There's always someone." She stalked over to the office and went in.

Gig took Ad by the arm and led him to a quiet corner for an intense conversation. No doubt about the future of this picture. Or what was left of it since the star was now in the process of being fingerprinted and locked up.

Quiet footsteps came from behind Beluga.

"Arrests for murder, a dying film, and poltergeist activity. I can see how being a biology professor is dull by comparison."

Beluga whirled toward the voice and caught the slender beauty in a tight bear hug. "Olivia! What are you doing here? I thought you weren't coming until tomorrow."

The young woman smiled. "And miss all this poltergeist activity? Not a chance."

"Let me see you," Beluga demanded.

Olivia turned, then curtsied. "Am I all you hoped for?"

"Absolutely not."

Olivia frowned and tightened as if for a battle.

"You're far more than I could have ever dreamed." Beluga beamed with pride and touched the corner of Olivia's lips until she smiled. "And what a looker you are. Hard to believe you took a sample from my gene pool. Must have been the chlorinated part."

"You haven't changed a bit, Mom."

Beluga feigned great hurt at this comment. "I have a whole new wardrobe. This delectable item I'm wearing is one of my best. You don't want to know what happened to the one I was wearing this morning."

Olivia scanned her mother's muumuu. "I see we've moved to domestic flora."

"Change now and then is good." Beluga grabbed her daughter for another hug and kissed her on both cheeks. "I missed you, baby. More than you'll ever know."

"I missed you too, Mom."

"Good. Then you won't mind if I permanently glue you to my side."

"People might talk."

"I certainly hope so."

They separated, cleared their throats, and found high interest in the floor as the conversation came to an awkward pause.

Beluga jumped with the sudden thought. "How did you know it was poltergeist activity that caused the light problems? I wasn't sure myself until just a moment ago."

"You forget who raised me."

"Not for a minute."

"And who insisted I live in a home filled with metaphysical and preternatural trappings."

"Guilty. An open mind is an enlightened one. Good work, my brilliant, intuitive daughter."

"Besides, it was you who put it all together. I just went along for the show." Olivia turned thoughtful. "Your Boley is a little older than most for a poltergeist, but I suppose that isn't completely out of line."

"He adores Buddy Holly and lives in a mansion with one room devoted exclusively to games and other amusements."

"A pool table?"

"Yes, dear. Why do you ask?"

"You didn't take him, did you, Mom?"

"I let him win."

Olivia laughed. "You have changed. And more than just your wardrobe."

Beluga reached into her pocket for the pack. "Cigarette?"

"I don't smoke."

"Good for you." She chose a green one, lit it, and inhaled deeply. "These things are filled with rat droppings and carbon monoxide. So I've been told. Repeatedly."

"Sounds like fun, but I'll pass."

Beluga blew smoke rings and eyed her daughter. "I need you, Olivia."

"I need you, too."

"You can't imagine how long I've waited to hear that, but it's not what I meant."

Olivia's eyebrows, so much like her mother's sharp point rather than a softer curve, shot up to her auburn bangs. "Oh?"

"It was a blast of fate that brought us together again. And with your uncanny ability to figure things out, maybe you can help me solve this case."

"This is a case?"

"Actually, it's a temp job, but someone had to do it."

"Somehow, I'm not surprised it was you. Well," Olivia drawled. "I was hoping you'd take me to the zoo, the park, and out for an ice cream now and then, but I suppose solving a murder can be just as interesting."

"Murders, dear. There were two of them."

"Oh, my. And I suppose that example of bad acting who was hauled away by the police is not on your top suspect list?"

"That's my baby. Right on both counts—the bad acting and the anti-suspect. Although I have no doubt, Jett

Blacke is on someone's list. Now walk with me while I fill you in on the details." Beluga took a deep drag on her cigarette, then dropped the butt into a prop honeycomb. She wrapped an arm around her daughter's shoulders. "So tell me, dear, are you still on good terms with that cute crime reporter?"

Beluga Stein's Diary

Having found an empty table in the restaurant set and away from the self-inflicted chaos of the remaining cast and crew, the three of us are busy at work. Well, two of us anyway. Olivia gratefully accepted Gig's director chair to carry out her new duties. I have settled, if not comfortably, at least tenuously into a discarded lawn chair.

Maybe it's just me, but it seems the chair was retrieved for the single purpose of determining if my weight would balance on the two remaining strips of green and white plastic. Someone around here has poor taste in humor. And a worse understanding of physics.

Rounding out our investigative troika is my dear familiar. Planchette has taken this quiet opportunity to curl up under the salad bar prop to catch some much-needed sleep and the occasional cockroach.

Dear, dear Olivia. Between words in my diary, I look at her beautiful face and thank the higher authorities for bringing my daughter back to me. She has my eyes, you know, my perfect cheekbones and a mind that's always working. Fortunately for her, she inherited her father's slender build and thus will never know the terror a disabled lawn chair can bring to one's self-esteem.

Sadly, she has also accepted the personality characteristics of stubbornness, a smart mouth, and an unyielding will stronger than iron.

I can't imagine where that comes from.

Still, I love her dearly. And when I'm confident that Olivia's here to stay, will never run away for two years without a letter or any other form of communication, and no indication of where she was—what, she couldn't pick up a phone now and then?—I will exert the law of mothers and threaten to kill her if she ever does it again. It is my right, and I stand by it.

Then, when the greatly anticipated loving argument and tears are over, I will inquire about her underwear status. Emergency Rooms are the same all over the world in that regard, and so are a mother's thoughts. I can't control that part of maternal territory.

But these are thoughts and plans for the future. Thankfully I have a future with my daughter right now. One can only hope there is a future for this picture after seeing the look on Gig's face. Her usual dynamic presence has been dampened and slowed by the unceasing onslaught of bad news and events. While a bee man can have a stand-in with the help of a spare costume, there is only one Jett Blacke. And, apparently, two murder victims who were effective in taking the one Jett Blacke off this picture for an indefinite time.

In the meantime, Boley Ash has been self-imprisoned in the film office with his new sidekick, Betty, the film editor. Undoubtedly, Boley is on the phone, caught in a fiber-optic mania, trying to pull every string he and his family have to spring Jett from her incarceration.

I wonder if Supreme Court justices turn on their answering machines this late in the evening. Or if they simply ruled against such devices.

I also can't help but speculate on film editor Betty's role in this state of confusion. She did make it clear, in her indomitable way, that she had helpful contacts all over the industry. Thus, she could pull strings easier than a puppet master holding a battalion of Balinese marionettes. Perhaps in this regard, Betty's role is to shore up Boley with an infusion of moral support. But I do have to wonder why we have been graced with her buxom presence lately.

Ah, but my daughter sighs as the phone headset becomes one with her ear. It would appear she, too, has been sucked into a fiber-optic nightmare of her own. I hope it's worth it, and she becomes as captivated with this murder problem as I have.

Chapter 16

"No, wait. Don't—" Olivia groaned and shifted the phone to her other ear. "I hate being put on hold. Hate it with every fiber of my being and ethical self. Two years in a Central American village and I didn't miss the phone one second."

Beluga pulled herself from her notes. "Central American?"

"Plumbing would have been nice, but you get used to living without it after a while."

"No plumbing? Foreign lands? Dear, is there something you should tell me?"

Olivia waved her hand and concentrated on the conversation that was coming through. "I see. Uh, huh. Yeah. Got it." She frowned, then shook her head. "Yeah, I owe you one, Squint. Uh, huh. Oh, you do, do you? And how exactly do I fit in with this particular fantasy?" She listened, then laughed. "In your dreams, lover boy. Yeah, right. Okay. Keep me posted. Talk to you soon." Olivia hung up and scratched a few notes on the back of a shooting schedule.

Beluga shifted in the lawn chair and felt the plastic strips drop an inch. "Well?"

"Just a sec."

"Lover boy? Fantasy? In your dreams? Not that this kind of talk isn't disconcerting in itself, but I trust you know our movie accountant frowns on calling 900 numbers. Unless, of course, it's strictly for business purposes. Honestly, he and Boley are such sticklers for details."

"Uh-huh."

"And since when does a call-in sex line name their employees 'Squint?'"

"When the person wears glasses with inch-thick lenses and was at one time considering the fascinating field of gastroenterology. The name was a joke, it stuck, and he prefers not to use it as a by-line on his crime stories. Get your mind out of the gutter, Mom."

"My mind is quite happy in the gutter, thank you. And I can't tell you how relieved I am to hear that you have chosen the way of the non-pervert."

"I didn't say that."

"You're killing me, Olivia."

"He's an old friend, happily married. But he is a big flirt, and he managed to call in a few favors to get information on Jett Blacke. Want to hear it?"

"Does Planchette have an ass?"

Planchette opened one eye and glared.

"Sorry, boy."

"Now, who's the pervert, Mom?"

"I am. Tell all." She leaned forward in the chair, felt the folded note in her pocket gouge her side, and pulled it out. Beluga listened while scanning the driver list of the pumpkin-orange car.

"The investigators found a packet of cocaine, cash, and Sander Siler's business card in Jett Blacke's trailer, not to mention copious impressions of his fingerprints. Apparently, the trailer was hauled off somewhere as useless after the door was peeled open by some rescue device?"

"Long story."

"She has a previous offense record for assault and battery, but the charges were dropped when the men in question refused to go along with it."

"Oh boy. But that doesn't explain a murder charge."

"Squint said the same thing. He also said large amounts of thin wire and latex pieces that match missing parts of a bee costume were found. I'm talking lots of stuff. Assorted mangled magazines used for sending threatening letters were all over the place. This includes particularly damning pages that graphically depict Sanders Siler's face glued onto a body of a bee while suspended high in the air, and the Bee Man rendered as a victim of garroting."

"That's bad. That's real bad."

"Worse is that someone made a statement to the police giving Jett Blacke a motive for the murders. Thus the reason for the arrest warrant."

"Really, really bad."

"It would seem your star is not a candidate for the Miss Congeniality Award either."

"You got that right, Olivia." Beluga ran her finger down the page of pumpkin-orange disaster car drivers.

It wasn't, as she had first thought, a random list of names given her by the young production assistant, but a meticulous record that monitored the comings and goings of his car and those at the wheel.

"No, Miss Congeniality, our Jett Blacke."

"In short, she's actively ticked off everyone downtown with her histrionics. The officials are not happy about it. They're pushing for her to be held without bond. And they've requested duct tape for her mouth."

"May God have mercy on those officials' souls. They

have their hands full with our illustrious star." Beluga strained in the poor light to stare at the list and gasped when she found it. "I'll be damned."

"What?"

"Right here, in black and white. Next to every one of Jett's signatures is a smiley face. Oh boy, oh boy, oh boy. But wait, this doesn't make a lot of sense."

"Mom," Olivia said, a tad exasperated. "This whole thing is too bizarre for words. Making sense would be a pleasant diversion."

Ad appeared from the depths of deep shadow. "Gig's calling a wrap. There's nothing more we can do on this picture tonight until we have the chance to regroup."

"Just the man I'd like to have a talk to," Beluga said, twisting in the lawn chair. "Stand by my feet if you will, Ad, since it would appear I'm doomed to eternity stuck in this aluminum bear trap. You've met my beautiful daughter, Olivia?"

Ad nodded appreciatively to Olivia.

"She's off-limits, by the way."

"Mom, don't start."

"It's just for the record, honey. Now then, Ad, about the letter you sent me—"

"I told you I didn't send it."

"Oh, that's right. You made it, but Jett sent it. Right?"

"She tried to scare you off. It's no secret she doesn't like you."

"The feeling is mutual, I assure you. But being hauled off to jail is amazingly effective in changing one's personality."

"Maybe." Ad's voice clearly indicated doubt. "Look, those stupid magazine things were showing up all over the place. I just tried to give Ashbole a dose of his own medicine so we could get on with work and forget about superstitious nonsense."

"What about the Bee Man?"

"What about him?"

"He started the magazine picture thing."

Ad shook his head. "I didn't know about that."

"But you're the assistant director." Beluga said.

"Yeah, for now. After this disaster, I'll be lucky to get a job flipping burgers."

"Are you a Director's Guild member?"

"No. This is a right-to-work state, and a non-union crew is cheaper. That means work is easier to come by if you're not a member."

"But you knew that Gig was a union member?"

"We all knew that."

"How did you feel about that, Ad?" Beluga stretched this next point since facts were not on her side. "She's getting paid more than you because of training, but you've racked up a few points in experience. Maybe even more than she has."

Ad hesitated in his answer. "This dog can still learn a few tricks. Besides, in this business, contacts are everything. I wouldn't jeopardize my future by being labeled a squealer. Word gets out."

"Would Jett tell someone about Gig?"

"Jett?" Ad rolled his eyes and sighed deeply. "Jett has her own ideas about everything. She didn't like Gig. She doesn't like anyone. But she respected Gig's talent. No, I don't think she would have squealed either."

"Did Jett like you, Ad?"

"At first. But then she became an onion."

"An onion? You mean the vegetable?"

"Yeah. The first layer was kinda spicy and fun, but the rest stunk and was rotten to the core."

Beluga grimaced. "My undying gratitude goes to you for that graphic image."

"I'm telling you the truth. I couldn't wait to get rid of her. But not enough to set her up for murder."

"You think it was a setup?"

"Yeah. Yeah, I do. She was nasty with the best of them but always to your face."

"Except for my recent letter."

"You weren't afraid of her. She had to do something to get you in line."

Olivia laughed. "That was a losing proposition."

"Enough from the peanut gallery," Beluga shot back.

"She even started the food fight on your first day and blamed you."

"So did you, I might add," Beluga said.

He shrugged. "Film baptism by snack food." Ad peered at his watch. "Look, if the interrogation is over, I got to get to a meeting to plan what we're going to do next."

"Sure, sure." Beluga shifted within the cloying grasp of the lawn chair, then slipped further into the depression that locked her hips in place. "Just one more thing."

"Make it quick."

"Where would Jett go if she had the use of a car between shooting scenes?"

"It wouldn't happen."

"Oh? And why not?"

"The transportation team takes the cast where ever they need to go. Besides, Jett doesn't drive. She never learned how."

Beluga opened her mouth to speak, but no words

were forthcoming with this new bit of information.

"Enough? I can go now?" Ad stared at the mute Beluga. "Okay. See you later. Nice to meet you, Olivia."

"Likewise."

Beluga stared at the driver's list, and a numbness clouded her mind. Jett Blacke didn't drive? Then whose smiley faces were those?

"Mom? Are you all right?"

No answer.

"You know," Olivia said, "I didn't miss the phone in the Central American village, and I was hot and cold on the lack of plumbing—I mean that literally—but the worst part was when I got overwhelmed by the problems. It was a forest for the trees thing, you know. I wanted to fix everything." She reached from her perch on the director's chair to stroke her mother's shoulder. "I guess what I'm saying is that you can't fix everything all the time."

"Damn. I didn't ask Ad about why he was at the special effects warehouse. I knew there was something else."

Anyway, it's the thought that counts. And the effort. Let's go home. Maybe we'll figure something out tomorrow."

Beluga's voice took a tight edge. "Don't patronize me with your mothering tactics. I'm a mother. I know those tactics. I've tried them on you, and they don't work. They most certainly will not play with me."

"I'm just trying to help," Olivia said with mock hurt. Her face changed instantly to barely concealed humor. "How about this, then? Well, you can sit there like a stump if you want to, but don't ask me to landscape around you."

"I never said that."

"Let me count the ways."

"No wonder you could hardly wait to leave me."

"It had nothing to do with you, Mom."

"I pushed you out of the nest."

"Yes. And to beat this metaphor to death, it was time for me to try my wings."

"You never called; you never wrote."

"Old joke, Mom. Ancient. But I get your drift. And I did write."

"Three times, if that. Even an alumni association couldn't find you with such a sketchy return address. Trust me, I asked. Those people could find Jimmy Hoffa if they thought he'd make a generous donation."

"I was angry, and I was remiss. But I've also grown up a bit. Forgive me?"

"For growing up? Never."

"You know what I mean."

"Yes, I do. But you don't get off the hook that easy."

"Oh? What do you have in mind?"

Beluga wriggled in the lawn chair. "You know, between captivating chairs and head molds, I'm thinking of a second career as a contortionist if this P.I. thing doesn't work out. But first, I have to find the smiley face artist, and you're going to help."

The working lights to the set winked out and threw them in total darkness.

"In other words," Olivia said, "you thought I could shed a little light on the matter."

"Well spoken, oh daughter of darkness."

In the distance, a door squealed open, releasing a tangle of frantic voices between Boley and film editor Betty. Furniture and props toppled to the floor.

The two sets of footsteps sounded hollow and panicked as they danced randomly in the dark to find a familiar place.

All over the soundstage, sets suddenly rattled and swayed as if gusts of wind had caught them on the high seas rather than in a contained building.

Planchette screeched, hissed, and dove into Beluga's lap. With a final high-pitched groan from plastic strips stretched to their breaking point, the lawn chair dumped its occupants squarely on the hard cement below.

Boley Ash's voice rose above the din and expletives and reverberated throughout the almost abandoned soundstage. "He's out. Max is out, and I can't stop him!"

Chapter 17

Boley had been right.

Max was indeed out. And the poltergeist was ticked.

The single, broad beam flashlight sat at the center of the restaurant set table. A wedge of upside-down, pyramid-shaped light was aimed toward the ceiling of the soundstage and captured four separate, grim silhouettes. Behind them, the building stood dark. And right now, Max was calling the shots.

Beluga sat solidly and with some modicum of comfort in Gig's director chair. The lone seat was an offering Olivia made and gratefully accepted by her bruised mother, who now looked from one face to another about the round table.

On the periphery of the table and surrounding shadow sat a stunned Olivia. Opposite her was Betty, who hadn't blinked for a half-hour, and clung to the table edge as if letting go would release demons from hell. Boley Ash opted to stand nearby. His seemingly ceaseless supply of adrenaline kept him hopping from one foot to another while drumming mindless tunes on the table edge.

Planchette leaned his full body weight against Beluga's feet. No amount of prodding, nudging, or downright foot swipes at his lean physique would persuade him to consider other options of still-life postures. He had long since grown quiet and very, very small, as if afraid of being noticed.

But Max had noticed.

He had noticed all of them. And it appeared the ghost was not happy.

Beluga ducked as a piece of cardboard swept over her by the howling wind creating more noise than an actual weather event. Still, personal injury was a possibility she'd rather avoid. Fortunately, her senses were still somewhat intact and could alert her to flying debris at the whim of a psychokinesis temper tantrum.

They had tried leaving the building with the aid of the found flashlight left by the construction crew on the previous hot set. Moving amoeba-like, they dodged flying materials, moaned as icy tendrils of air touched their faces, and jumped over small props rolling across the floor like tumbleweeds. And they had almost made it to one of the exit doors. Almost. It was then Max had made his disapproval clear. The exits had locked with a heart-stopping *clunk,* and the keys wrenched from Boley's hand then tossed by a strong gust somewhere within the cavernous dark.

Now the four of them gathered in a frightened clump on the restaurant set, waiting like sitting ducks for the hunter to reload.

Doors within the building slammed shut, then opened to slam again. Set furniture skittered across floors to bump into walls. Desk drawers opened, and the pencils and pens inside rattled around.

The craft services cart rolled back and forth, crashed into lighting trees, then fell over to spill its contents. Apples and oranges rolled in random directions; candy bars shed their wrappers and stuck to each other in gooey gobs; potato chips took to the air like lost feathers. Juice and soft drink cans popped their tops, and a lone salt container rolled to stop near their feet.

Beluga took a deep breath and yelled, "This is like every bad séance movie I've ever seen. All we need is a floating trumpet."

Boley covered his ears and froze. He scanned the dark as if afraid Beluga's statement would turn to instant fact.

"If we were shooting a musical tribute to jazz, you could worry. No trumpets here. In fact," she yelled, "I'd be relieved to see a trumpet. Then I'd know this was all a colossal fake or a bad special effects joke."

He lunged for the phone near Beluga's chair and thrust it at her.

"Who you gonna call?" she shouted. "And what would you say if they could hear you?"

The phone dropped limp from his hand. "Do something."

"It's your manifestation, Boley. *You* do something."

He shrugged helplessly then collapsed at her feet next to Planchette. A rolled rug in one corner unfolded itself toward him. Cringing in fear, then spurred to sudden motivation, he kicked at it, then pummeled the nap with his fists. "Stop it! Stop it right now! I can't take it anymore."

And it stopped.

All of it. The wind, the howls, and the kinetic activity.

But Boley didn't. His fury only increased as his fists beat the rug into quiet submission. He wailed at the rug, screamed his disapproval, then leaned over and bit it.

"It's over, Boley," Beluga said. "For now. Although I dare say, the carpet may never be the same after your taste test." She closed her eyes and rubbed tension out of her face.

This was not her idea of a fun evening. But at least it was interesting.

The phone rang. Four people and one cat stared. No one moved to answer it.

"I think someone should get that," Olivia said.

"I think you're right," Beluga said. "Get it, Boley."

He turned to her incredulously. "I'm not getting it. You get it."

Betty pried her fingers loose from the table and mustered action. "Give me the damn phone. Whoever it is can get us the hell out of this place. Hello. Yeah. Just a sec." She thrust the phone at Beluga, "It's for you. Some German lady."

Beluga groaned and answered the call. "Not now, Tanya. It's not a good time. *Blumen und weiss* wine. How nice. And they're tulips to boot, but...who? Not *the* Chuck Masters of Magic and Madness Special Effects. Did you find out anything?"

An unnatural shriek in the distance sounded and turned to a low keen.

The hair on Beluga's forearms stood on edge. A tingling started at the base of her neck and traveled her spine.

"M-mom?" Olivia's voice quavered. "I-I think it's happening again."

Boley Ash curled into the fetal position on the rug and covered his head.

"Gotta go, Tanya. We're in the midst of a ghost fest. So listen fast. Call Gig, and get the keys to this funhouse. We're trapped and—"

The phone rose into the air, hovered briefly, and threw itself across the room where it splintered into plastic pieces.

Then it rang.

Beluga stared at the handset she still gripped and the wire that dangled from it. Color drained from her face as she raised what was left of the phone to her ear and listened. A moment passed. Two.

"I think I just reached out and touched someone."

The restaurant table rumbled and bounced. The flashlight fell over on one side and shot a beam of light toward the giant beehive prop.

Olivia threw herself into her mother's arms, then looked around in alarm. "Where's Betty?"

Beluga swallowed hard and scanned the room as best she could. "She was here a minute ago. I'm sure of it."

The howling started again.

And then the screams. Human screams.

"Betty!" the two women shouted.

"Grab the flashlight, Olivia. Try to shine it around so she can get back to us."

Olivia did as she was told, but her hands shook so badly that Beluga feared for the future of the only light source.

Dust stirred and turned into a funnel-shaped cloud that danced and teased as it slowly made its way to them.

"Get under the table," Beluga shouted. She grabbed Planchette and rolled Boley under the table with her.

The flashlight beam stilled on the funnel that approached. Olivia's face turned hard as stone, her gaze fixed and unseeing. She didn't move. It didn't look like she could move.

"Olivia!"

The young woman didn't seem to hear. Her auburn hair whipped around her face. Her clothes tore as the leading edge of the dust tornado touched them. Tiny bits of solid matter scratched her face, creating bloody pinpoints.

Beluga's sudden panic turned her muscles to jelly. She tried to crawl, but her legs folded under her weight. Calling out, begging and pleading, her voice fell short in the powerful wind that kicked up around her.

She closed her eyes and called upon what strength she had left. Words of hope and requests for intervention formed on her lips. Her daughter had come back to her, and she would not let this or anything else come between them. Nothing would separate them again. Not from this plane or any other.

A rumble started in Beluga's chest and bubbled up to her throat. Her body shook with newfound energy and the undying love of an angry, protective mother. A scream of rage burst from her lips. Rocketing out from under the table like a fast-forward study in human evolution, from stooped to erect and powerful, she tackled her daughter and dragged her to safety. With the flashlight still held tight in her daughter's rigid grasp, she sheltered Olivia with her body as the storm encompassed their meager refuge.

Beluga spotted the escaped salt container rolling this way and that in the beam of fixed light and planned her next strategy.

The table over them buckled and cracked. The wood screeched and released stiletto-like splinters into the air. A table leg wobbled and wrenched free of most of the nails holding it in place.

"Stay here," Beluga ordered.

Fear dried her mouth to dust. Drawing breath as deep as worry allowed, she stroked her daughter's cheek then kissed it. She picked up the now flaccid Planchette and dropped him into the crook of Olivia's arm, then dragged the salt container closer to her with her foot.

The funnel cloud turned its attention on the salad bar.

Beluga recognized the opportunity and snatched up the salt, then bolted to the back of the warehouse. Within seconds she passed the outer limits of the light and plunged into a dark labyrinth of sets, props, equipment, and debris.

Remember where you are. Remember the layout of the building. Think. She tripped over something and fell hard on her knees. Cursing, she rose and tried again. She closed her eyes, visualized the building, and fine-tuned her keen senses. One step. Another.

There was something.

She toed the space ahead of her. Yes. A chair.

"It figured," she muttered. When you don't need one, there it is. And to her right, yes, the living room set. That means the back wall should be about...

Her forehead cracked solidly against the wall. She groaned, rubbed the sore place, then opened the salt container. Filling her hand with as much salt as she could hold, she sprinkled it about the area and whispered special words under her breath.

The wind picked up. The howling became the sound of fingernails on a chalkboard.

A woman's scream on the other side of the building was cut short.

Beluga traversed the length of the wall repeating the salt exercise, then stepped forward into a room to start the process again. She dodged converging furniture pieces as they scraped across the floor and heard two-by-fours that vibrated and hummed when she passed. Nearby tools turned on and started to work independently of human hands. The buzzing of bee prop paraphernalia suggested real hymenopterous activity. Beluga shuddered and continued on her personal mission.

This would work. This had to work. There was nothing else in her bag of tricks.

And when she got to the other end of the building, what then? How could this poltergeist be released? The doors were locked, and the keys were hidden somewhere in the mess.

She'd worry about that later.

Salt fell from her hand. She refilled her palm and continued. Something stopped her. It was heavy. Oppressive. Creepy.

And it wasn't a wall.

In fact, it was anything but physically tangible. She inhaled deeply and let the pictures in her mind form the story. Her gut tightened; bile rose in her throat. A glimmer. A tiny thread wove its way through the developing mental picture. Suddenly a fractured piece of the puzzle fell into place, and she knew. Without a doubt, she knew.

Betty's strangled cry reverberated through the building and pulled Beluga back to the task at hand. Salt sprayed in all directions. She spoke her special words quickly and moved on.

Passing the giant beehive prop humming with activity, she skirted the spilled craft services cart where pretzels shattered on the floor, and the slap of meat and cheese created sandwiches without benefit of consumers. Then ever so carefully, she approached the film office door.

There, in the dark, Beluga heard the muffled

whimpers. She ran her hand along the wall and stopped at the closed door to the office. "Betty?"

The whimpering stopped.

"Betty, it's me."

Beluga tried the doorknob. It was cold. Icy cold. She turned the knob with the hem of her muumuu. The door opened. A howl of protest floated on the wind and flew into the office.

Betty screamed. "Get away from me! Get out!"

Beluga flung salt in the room and whispered the words under her breath.

"Make it stop," Betty wailed.

The staccato beat of her high heels on the cement floor turned fast, faster until a brief, ominous quiet emerged from the dark to slam Beluga against the open door. Betty moaned when she hit the floor, righted herself, and bolted into the depths of the warehouse.

A bone-cold chill swept through Beluga and caught her breath. She gagged, tried to cough, but no air would move in or out of her lungs. Dizziness clouded her mind and brought with it a growing darkness inside. Then just as suddenly, her breath released, and she gasped for welcome new air.

The door at the front of the warehouse rattled. Pounding sounded from outside. Beluga staggered toward the noise, panting for breath and sprinkling salt at every step. The lock to the door twisted with a *clank* and opened. Chattering voices competed with each other as people spilled into the building. Someone's lighter cast a weak light into the immediate area, then winked out with the unnatural wind.

"Stand away from the door," Beluga ordered. "*Now*."

The small gathering shuffled back. She whispered the

special words one last time, tossed salt in the last space, then waited.

The howling shifted and twisted as if trying to find an acceptable pitch. It rose an octave, another, then shrieked in outrage and indignation.

Beluga dropped the salt container and covered her ears. The sound whipped around her, through her, and dug deep into her mind. She fought against it and felt its sudden release.

Max turned dense, almost solid while hovering at the unlocked front door. Then with a final wail, Boley's poltergeist was sucked out the door as if by a giant vacuum.

Something else followed Max out: a human form. A woman. Running out the door and across the parking lot, she was little more than a frightened shadow darting from one street lamp to another.

Perhaps this was the last they'd ever see of film editor Betty.

"Cigarette, anyone?" Beluga asked the small crowd.

A lighter fired up.

She watched the flame dance and sway, leaned heavily against the wall, and slid into a heap on the floor.

Chapter 18

"Coming through." The slight woman, wearing a tool belt over her coat and teddy bear pajamas, pushed past the small group sitting outside the door to the soundstage. "A body in the duct system again?" she asked, sans emotion.

"At last. Help has arrived," Beluga announced while drawing deeply on an orange cigarette. "No body, but we could use a little light in the building."

"Be still, Beluga," Tanya warned. "This compress won't stay on your head if you keep bobbing around like that."

"No can do," the tool-belt woman said. "This place was on its final *ohm* last time I took a look-see. Maybe I can rig a generator setup or something."

"Do try. It would be most helpful. Tanya, please take your Nightingale efforts elsewhere. You're giving me a headache."

Tanya pursed her lips. "That ostrich egg on your forehead is giving you the headache. I am merely trying to help. Trust me; I will not stay where I'm not wanted. So my ministrations and I will turn elsewhere, perhaps to someone who is appreciative and gracious. You're up, Olivia."

Olivia sat down at the makeshift first-aid station Tanya had created in the parking lot. "You were great in there, Mom."

"It was nothing." Beluga lit another cigarette off the

one she just finished.

"No, it was something all right. You saved us, and I'll never forget it."

Tanya cleared her throat.

"You, too, Auntie Tanya. You were great, too."

"Yeah," Beluga droned. "It took a colossal feat of courage to make a few phone calls and unlock the front door. With the help of Gig and Ad, I might mention."

"Watch it, Beluga," Tanya warned. "I have antiseptic wound spray, and I know how to use it."

"Are they still creeping around the soundstage?"

"Yes. They're in there. Along with your friend, Ashley—"

"Boley."

"—whoever. The three are surveying the interior damage inflicted by your little supernatural friend. I hear it's extensive. Security Bill is scrutinizing everything out here." Tanya cocked her head and adopted a conspiratorial tone. "Now then, vast amounts of praise and lavish attention is a small price to pay if you want to hear all about my date tonight."

"You're still dating, Auntie Tanya?"

"As hard as it is to believe, Olivia, she's dating. But tonight, it was something a little different." Beluga took a deep drag and blew it out. "It's a rare night in her social calendar when Tanya doesn't have a date—"

"Tell it," Tanya said.

"But tonight, she had other plans. And, by the way, Olivia, she's not your aunt." Where were those stupid lights? Surely a generator would be up and running by now.

"We have a special relationship, Olivia and I," Tanya said. "Don't we, dear? And I won't have a tired, grumpy ghost fighter spoil it for us. So, from this moment on, I have decided not to speak to your mother anymore until she's in a better mood." She dabbed antiseptic on Olivia's wounds. "So, my dear, it was like this. Chuck Masters, of special effects local fame, found me immediately attractive while I was engaged in a covert diversion activity."

"Diversion activity?"

"Yes, sweetie."

"Covert?"

"Of course. Another of my many gifts, dear."

Beluga harrumphed.

"Olivia, dear, do remind your mother I'm not speaking to her. Nor should she make any rude noises in my direction."

"Mom—"

"I heard."

Tanya folded up a gauze pad and aimed it at Olivia's face. "Hold still while I get this one nasty little place. Anyway, as I was saying, the covert diversion activity occurred after the head mold but before the parrot-puppet death. That was about when your mother chose to snoop around."

"I think Mom forgot to tell me that part."

"I'm sure. Anyway, I led Chuck to believe that I was a producer on a big, really big, film project that would involve lots of special effects. Expensive special effects. Well, of course, he bought it hook, line, and lead weight. Who wouldn't after one look at me?"

"Spare us the editorial, and get on with it." Beluga crushed the cigarette out under her foot. C'mon with the lights already. A working phone would be nice, too. She tapped her foot impatiently.

"Okay, you're done. Planchette, you're up."

The cat jumped to the table and sat passively under Tanya's scrutinizing eye. She stroked his body, squeezed his legs, and ran her hand over his tail.

"You're clean. Next."

Planchette yowled at her.

"Oh, sorry, big guy." Tanya reached into her purse and pulled out a package of cat treats.

The cat eyed the bag a split second, then grabbed it with his teeth and jumped off the table.

"A tad hungry, were we? I suspected that might be the case. See, I can learn a few tricks, too," she said to Beluga over her shoulder.

"The story, Tanya."

"Yes, of course. Anyway, there we were. Nice corner restaurant table. A bouquet of tulips sitting next to my plate. White wine in my glass. A double whiskey in his fourth glass, but who's counting?"

"I'm getting testy." Time was whipping by, and she had things to do. Where was everybody?

"*Tut mir leid.* I'm sorry, already. Did you know he gets a little sloppy after a few drinks? And a tad grabby, I'm glad to add."

"*Tanya.*"

"Anyway, he admits it has been a bad day after a really bad week. Business, in general, has been poor. The IRS is breathing down his neck for back taxes, and, get this, a large pay-off from a client has mysteriously disappeared."

"Your point?"

"Didn't you hear me? He said 'pay-off,'' not 'payment.' One might find that a bit suspicious."

Beluga sat up. "I certainly do."

"As did I. And the visitor was a woman as you thought, wearing high heels. Sadly, he didn't drink enough to reveal her name or other pertinent information, except that she's involved with a local film." Tanya reached for her purse to apply another layer of blood-red lipstick. "He did, however, mention talking to the police at great length yesterday. Batting eyelashes, a few questions, and even picking up the tab—you owe me eighty-seven bucks, by the way—got me zip on why he talked to the police and what he said." She patted her lips with a tissue, then wiped the corners of her mouth. "I did the best I could."

Beluga leaped to her feet and wrapped her arms around Tanya. "Olivia was right. You're great."

"I was, wasn't I? So why the sour mood, *liebe* Beluga?"

"I got another feeling when I was in there," she said, nodding toward the soundstage.

"Mind pictures, too?"

"Yeah. Strong ones. Pretty vivid. Now I'd like to check it out with a little light." Beluga tiptoed to the soundstage door and peered in. "Then there's the phone call I got when we were in there."

"I called you."

"Yes, you did. But the event to which I am referring was after your call and probably wouldn't be approved by the FCC." Beluga shuddered at the thought, then paced the parking lot in front of the door. "And if it all checks out like I'm sure it will, there's another call or two I need to make tonight. The usual way this time." She stopped at the door. "I've put this off long enough. Cover me. I'm going in."

"Mom, are you sure it's gone? The ghost?"

"Yeah, no doubt about it." At least she hoped that was true. There weren't enough cigarettes in a convenience store hold-up to get her through another experience like the last one.

"You don't mind if I stay out here, do you, Mom?"

"I'll keep an eye on her. No sense in her being alone. It looks like Planchette will defer this excursion as well."

"Have it your way." Beluga stepped into the building and breathed deep of the air.

On the cool side, but that was little surprise since the heating system was weak at best. It felt empty as well, and that was good. No sign of a supernatural presence that had read *The Tempest* one too many times.

And it was dark. There was no sign of Boley, Gig, or Ad.

"Helloooo."

No answer. She flicked the lighter and, deciding not to waste it, lit a cigarette. Tobacco was little use as a weapon, but a deep drag now and then did wonders to numb frayed nerves.

She inched forward and stepped on something uneven. It jingled under her weight and threw her off balance. Catching herself, she then bent over and touched the thing. Boley's keys. The very set the ghost had flung from the producer's grasp now found a safe place in her pocket. She'd transfer them to her purse for safe keeping until they were given back to Boley.

Retracing her steps to the place where the visions occurred, she stood in shadow and closed her eyes.

The pictures arrived more forcefully this time, one after another, like deep, rhythmic punches to her gut. She grunted with the impact but held her ground to watch the scenes play out.

Faster and faster, the onslaught of pictures and connecting emotion drove her back a step and finally broke her concentration.

She fell back into the dark and released her held breath. Tears sprung to her eyes at the victim's feelings of despair and pain when the murderous act was carried out. These same feelings now washed over Beluga like an emotional photocopy of the original event.

The murder had been planned and executed in a cold-blooded, calculated way. The killer had been slow in bringing about death and relished the agony inflicted on the victim. Beluga shuddered. The energy was bad here.

And it was definitely not that of Jett Blacke.

She wiped her eyes with the back of her hand and lit a cigarette that sat on her lips next to the previous one. The flame from the lighter created a small circumference of light. She inhaled, blew blue smoke upwards, and released the lighter lever. The flame remained and burned bright.

Beluga felt it first, then looked up.

His face shimmered in the glow of peripheral flame and smoke. The bushy eyebrows that seemed to join in the middle wrinkled in concern and worry. His eyes held fear. And a plea.

She gasped.

An engine rumbled, and the working lights to the building kicked in to emit a dull, yellow glow.

The lighter winked out, and with it, the shimmering face of Sanders Siler, the Bee Man.

Her hand went to her throat. She coughed with the tightness that settled there and stared at the object beyond the point of the Siler vision. The SFX crane.

The crane looked like little more than antique farm

equipment but was nothing less than sturdy. Rust covered its once-painted surface, and the gears last appeared to have been oiled decades ago.

Gig appeared behind her. "You surprise me."

Beluga jumped. "And you just turned my bowels to spaghetti." She sighed and fanned herself. "Geez. Couldn't you let a person know you were coming?"

"What? In these?" Gig picked up one foot clad in a hiking boot and pointed. "Good support. And quiet. Perfect for shooting a film. Not like there is a film anymore."

"Quiet, you say? Not like, say, high heels?"

"No, not like those at all."

"Do you wear high heels, Gig?"

"I've been known to. A woman still has to play the game now and then, male business being what it is. My lone pair is with a pile of clothes in the projector room. Emergency stash since I'm almost always there, if not here."

"I see."

"Why?" She eyed Beluga's feet. Her forehead creased. "Do you want to borrow them or something?"

"No. No. Nothing like that."

"Oh, good. I mean, why the sudden interest in footwear after the experience you had tonight? You've surprised me by coming back into this building."

"Do you believe in ghosts, Gig?"

"I'm beginning to."

Beluga pointed to the SFX crane. "Can you show me how this works?"

"Not a clue. Ad can do it."

"But you can't?"

"Male business again. At least in this case. I tried and

couldn't make it budge. I was never very clear on how it worked anyway." Gig pointed to a large crank. "Ashbole wouldn't spring for hydraulics. Too expensive. We made do with a crank and testosterone-backed upper body strength."

"Could Jett Blacke have turned that crank?"

"And break a fingernail? I don't think so. I think I know where you're going with this. Siler was killed and hauled up by the crane. Jett couldn't have possibly done it."

"That's what I'm thinking. At the very least, she couldn't have done it by herself. My gut tells me she didn't do it at all." Beluga looked to the top of the machine, the chains, and the hook. "It was someone with muscle. Someone with little regard for others. Little enough regard, anyway, that he could take a life and leave the body here to be easily discovered. It was more than a murder. It was a message as well." She stroked her chin. "Maybe one of a series of messages. Is there a working phone somewhere? I'd rather not try the one on the restaurant set again if you don't mind."

"Boley! We need you." Gig shouted. "Since your ordeal tonight, he hasn't released a finger from his cellphone once he got it out of his car. Of course, we had a few doubts that we'd be able to get *him* out of the car." Gig strolled toward the front of the building.

Beluga followed while listening closely to the rhythm of the director's footsteps. Was Gig the one in the special effects office? Could she be involved in a "pay-off?" Beluga's headache escalated with the mental storm of questions. The answers were here. Here, in this very building like the bodies had been. And the magazine cut-outs. And the ghosts.

Boley's manifested ghost, Max, and now the ghost of Sanders Siler.

Ad followed Boley around the craft services cart debacle, kicking fruit out of the way. "It's over, Ashbole. The picture is gone. Finished. Dead."

The red-faced Boley covered his ears with his hands and cellphone, aimlessly humming between sentences. "I'm not listening to you. I can't hear you."

"Well, you better listen." Ad grabbed Boley by his starched, white shirt collar and yanked the producer close to his face. "We have no star. We have no bee. We have nothing." He dropped Boley to his knees. "It's a wrap."

"No, I won't allow it."

Ad sneered. "You won't allow what?" He stomped around the fallen producer. "You've seen the sets. This place is a mess. And the electrical system, what's left of it, is being run by spit and chewing gum. Once the few crew left hears about tonight, you can bet your last phone call to Daddy they won't be back." He kicked his boot-clad foot into the overturned craft cart, spinning it. "It's over. Let it go."

"He's right, Boley," Gig said. "I don't see any way we can get this picture in the can. I'll be back here bright and early in the morning to see what's salvageable, but don't hold your breath."

Beluga went to the producer and stroked his head. "I'm sorry. Really. I know how much this meant to you. Now give me your phone."

Boley eyed her. "What are you going to do with it?"

"I'm going to dust the set with it. Make a call, of course. What else would I do?"

He handed it to her, and she punched a series of numbers. "Hey. It's me." She rolled her eyes. "Yes, I know what time it is. Well, actually, I don't, but this couldn't wait. Darwin…Darwin. Will you stop complaining and listen a minute?"

The young producer pulled himself from the floor and stalked toward the office. Ad continued his mutilation of fruit while Gig stood by and watched.

"You heard about Jett Blacke? On the news, huh? Well, she didn't do it… I'm sure."

Ad stopped his manic activity and joined Gig in staring.

"No, I don't have any proof. Any acceptable in our archaic investigation system, anyway. But you do." Beluga nodded impatiently and waved her hand. "Well, the old goat ME—say hi to him for me, if you would—will just have to make time. Darwin, will you please stop prattling on and listen? Are you calm now? Good."

She looked at Ad and Gig, then shrugged. "Check the Bee Man's hands, Darwin. I think you'll find some interesting evidence that may just get Jett Blacke off the hook. Yes, I know you're very thorough. Yes, I know you've done everything by the book. Darwin, listen to me. *Darwin*. Please, for me. Take another look… You will? Great. Oh, and Darwin, was the Bee Man in pretty good shape?" Beluga made a face. "No, I don't mean now. I'm perfectly aware of his current condition. I mean before… Uh-huh. Strong enough to hoist a man in the air with the aid of a rusted crank on old farm equipment used as a special effects crane?"

Beluga turned away and whispered into the phone, "You can leak that last little bit of info to the police, by the way. Uh-huh. I see. Thanks. I know you'll get right on it. What's that?" She laughed. "I won't live that long to pay you back. See you, Darwin."

She turned off the phone and looked from Ad to Gig. "Well, that's taken care of. Now, if the investigators are worth their pay, they'll figure it out, too."

"The Bee Man was a body builder," said Gig.

"The steroids helped," Ad said. "He even offered them to me, along with a few other not–quite-legal drugs."

"Yeah," Gig added. "He was pretty unhappy that his body was hidden by a bee costume for most of the film. So you think he killed Siler?"

"That's a real possibility."

"Then who killed him?" Gig asked.

Beluga shook her head. "I only wish I knew. Maybe Jett. Maybe someone else." She paused and studied the director. "Any ideas, Gig?"

"None, I'm afraid."

"Me, too. I'm through with your phone, Boley. Boley?" Beluga eyed the office door and the ashen Boley, who clung there as if afraid to move. "Don't tell me there's something else."

Boley nodded weakly and cocked his head to the office.

"I'm getting too old for this," Beluga said as she drifted tentatively to the office. "If it's another body, I really will insist I get benefits, along with a raise." She peered in, became immediately transfixed, and stumbled into the room.

They were everywhere. The room was covered by them like bad wallpaper at the hands of a crazed decorator. And this time, the energy was most definitely feminine.

Sticky notes, each bearing a smiley face, grinned at her from every inch of the office.

Chapter 19

No one could stop her now. Not even Beluga Stein.

She glanced through the pages of the shooting script and calculated the percentage of film completed and that outstanding.

The cast and crew would never reach the traditional Champagne toast at the one-hundredth reel of film. The small landmark for celebration was just shy of being reached, and she could pat herself on the back for a job well done as a result.

Of course, the Bee Man had been instrumental in this cause when he murdered Sanders Siler. It was a cause Win Rainey, the Bee Man, was only barely aware of, but one that had succeeded in spite of his greed and inflated ego. Or maybe it was because of his personality attributes. If you could call what he had a personality. He was an overbearing, control type game-player who lost the game when his twinge of conscience kicked in. The wire was far more effective around his neck than in his antennae.

It was easy to spot a defect, a weakness of will and spirit, a mile away, and she didn't hesitate to use it against an unsuspecting victim for her own gain. And there were so many unsuspecting victims. Especially in the movie business. One could throw a stick into a crowd and hit a hopeful star or someone who wanted to get their hands just a little bit dirty in the picture-making world. They'd work sweeping floors on a soundstage if they thought there was a glimmer of hope in being discovered. Or they'd clean up after the lunch break. Sometimes they'd even fill in as the bee aunt.

Anything for attention and their coveted fifteen minutes of fame. Even if it meant stirring up trouble under the guise of supernatural stirrings.

She shivered. Tonight had been a mess. Something she hoped she'd never have to deal with again during her film career. And for a moment, rationalized away now by the light and warmth of her secure apartment, she had believed in the possibility of ghosts. The disaster on the set had laid claim to the possibility.

But there was no such thing as ghosts. And unlike Win Rainey, there was no need for a conscience. Such simple-minded drivel. There was, however, the need for psychic investigators. The one had been quite useful, as it turned out. Important in assuring the demise of a film already weakened by superstition.

Always willing to share credit where credit was due, she acknowledged thanks to the unchecked egos who fueled turf fighting to greater heights via pictures glued to paper. Fear of ghostly doings had been around long before she nudged it to new panicked heights. Things had turned out quite well.

Chuck Masters and his bag of tricks couldn't be praised enough for help in setting the stage of evidence. Or for his carefully rehearsed statement to the police. But he had been paid handsomely for his talent, so they were even-steven.

And with Jett Blacke, the queen of narcissists and poor acting, in jail at this very moment, things couldn't be better.

Only now had the sweetness of revenge begun as far

as settling the score with Jett. It had taken hard work, study, and fighting her way up the political ladder of filmmaking while cultivating important contacts. And it had taken a great deal of time.

It was almost worth it.

She had reached her limit with ego-fueled actresses in general, and specifically with that one. A difficult childhood had become a nightmare of epic proportions, thanks to Jett's constant bullying and self-serving tricks. So when Jett Blacke memorized the number on her prison uniform because movie roles had dried to dust, then, and only then, would revenge be complete.

Until that happened, she had to settle for lesser things. A film in ruins; a young man with delusions of producing because of his parents' money, now returning to the basement mailroom where he belonged; and a particularly nasty, drug-and-deal-making Bee Man void of personality who found his niche in an air conditioning duct.

And then there was Beluga Stein. Something needed to be done about her nosy inquiries, and soon.

Things couldn't be better. But they could get worse, a lot worse, if Beluga Stein kept butting in where she had no business being. The cow. If the nasty, oh so narcissistic, despicable woman of muumuus, cigarette lighters, mangy cats, a worthless daughter, and snack cart destruction ever decided to rise above that charlatan act of hers; she might just be able to figure out the truth.

Then things could get much, much worse.

But that wouldn't happen. There was too much at stake. She had worked far too long and hard to let anybody stand in her way. Fame was way overdue, and fifteen minutes not near long enough for the risks taken.

She smiled.

It wasn't over until the fat psychic sang.

She scribbled on a sticky note, then punctuated it with a smiley face.

Chapter 20

Much needed sleep had been elusive for Beluga. She tossed and turned and fought with the bed sheets until she thought they'd strangle her like a particularly difficult and confused linen boa constrictor.

Counting sheep hadn't worked as she found herself mentally checking off their vital anatomy components. A review of sheep muscular systems forced her out of bed and into the kitchen, where she considered a glass of warm milk to quell the insomnia. It was then she remembered the broken refrigerator. The appliance had taken care of making the milk and everything else warm when it uttered its last gasp days ago.

Reluctantly she decided to take a pass on prematurely solidifying dairy products. It was the right thing to do.

A mother's habits never changed, so restless but exhausted, she checked on Olivia. Then she went back to bed and systematically removed Planchette from her pillow, one claw at a time, one vocal note up the octave at each claw removal.

He stared briefly, licked a paw, yawned, and then promptly curled up on her chest after she got settled.

Beluga didn't deny him the little luxury after a day like this but found sleep eluded her again. To pass the time, she counted his breaths, her breaths, then their breaths together until she thought she'd go mad or quit breathing altogether just for a break in the monotony.

There was nothing else but to review the day's events until the preceding dates merged and separated and formed again in confused scenarios and blurred faces.

She hadn't known sleep had arrived when she watched Jett Blacke serve spumoni with a spatula. And never before had dreams been as strange as the ones that followed Jett's.

Ad wore a bee costume that suddenly became a disaster of an orange car floating above the city skyline, only to land in a liquid pool of latex that formed a zombie head. The head turned, smiled, and tried to speak but spewed dollar bills rather than information.

A puppet parrot swung on its perch, cocked its head, and looked at her with Betty's face. "With these," parrot Betty said, pointing at her chest, "you can have anything you want. Trust me."

High heels, sans feet, and a body to direct them, tap-danced across the table top in the restaurant set.

Magazine cut-outs floated among the candy bars and fruit on the snack cart and landed in the form of an arrow at the base of an air conditioning duct. The vent shifted and bent to the form of a smiley face.

Sticky notes shimmered in gray shadow and fell like rain. Then a storm. Then a funnel cloud stole the breath out of her lungs.

"Mom?"

She jolted awake. "Huh? What is it?"

"You were snoring."

"Not possible," Beluga said, shaking her head in the hopes her mind would clear. "I haven't gotten a wink of sleep all night."

"Well, you were sleeping now."

"No, I just looked like I was sleeping."

"And you just acted like you were snoring for effect?"

"Yes. I mean, no."

"You were moaning too, Mom. It scared me."

Beluga lifted one corner of the comforter and waved to Olivia. "Climb in. It's cold. There now, that's better. Just move Planchette if he hogs too much space."

"He's not here."

"Oh. I guess he's having a little late-night snack or something."

Olivia snuggled to her mother. "You okay?"

"Couldn't be better. You?"

"The same." Olivia sighed. "What am I saying? I feel awful. Tonight scared the stuffing out of me. If I had a silver bullet, garlic, a mirror, a stone with an eye on it, holy water, a white candle, braided grass for smudging, and every religious medallion ever made, it wouldn't be enough."

"You wouldn't be very mobile either."

"Exactly. And on top of that, we're trying to find a murderer. You know, earlier tonight, I thought it would be kinda fun. But it's not a game, Mom. People have been killed."

Beluga yawned. "It's a challenge."

"It's the pits."

"I see your point."

"Why don't you let the police handle this?"

"They are handling it, in their way. I'm merely filling in the gaps."

"Let *them* fill in the gaps."

"They don't know how, Olivia."

"And you do?"

Her daughter had a way of direct questioning that

made Beluga proud. And a little nervous. When things were pointed out in such a concrete way, she had to grudgingly admit that maybe her working hypothesis wasn't as solid as she'd hoped.

"I like to think I can offer something. A different perspective at the very least, and a little insight into the people around me that might be overlooked by rote fact-finding."

"Insight?" Olivia asked, with a hint of sarcasm. "On people. What kind of insight, specifically?"

"I don't know. Part intuition, mixed with a cup of behavioral observation and a dash of questioning that catches them off guard."

"Mother, people are not recipes to be shared with members of The Ladies League."

Beluga cringed at her daughter's use of the word "mother." This was a disapproving term that only came into use when Olivia was unhappy about something and was indecisive about sharing the disapproval.

She reached out to tug the chain on the bedside lamp. Muted yellow light flooded her side of the bed and cast shadows about the room. Beluga sat up and punched the pillow behind her for a little support; doubtless, the only thing that would offer a buttress for the ensuing conversation that she knew was coming. The verbal dance with her daughter was quite familiar, even after Olivia's absence of two years, and it was another habit that never went away.

"Olivia, I'm sorry if I, in any way, implied that my work was yours as well. I accepted this job, and you are free to do as you will."

"You missed the point as usual, Mother."

Puberty had long since come and gone, the surly

teenage years were behind her, and Beluga was at a total loss to guess what phase her daughter was entering now. It didn't look good. And even though patience was a virtue, she had failed to stock up on it the first time around. She hoped she could muster a vague semblance of a virtue.

"You're right, Olivia. I don't have a clue what you're talking about."

"See," she said indignantly. "That's what I'm talking about."

"It is?"

"Yes."

"Oh." Beluga reached for a cigarette from the bedside table and lit it. "As much as I hate to admit this, I still don't know what you're talking about."

"You're hopeless, Mother. Absolutely hopeless."

"Until I know the topic, I think you're right."

"Just forget it."

"I would, but I have to know what it is to forget."

"That's what I mean."

"At least give me a hint. I'll wing it from there."

Olivia turned away and disappeared into shadow.

Beluga took deep drags from the cigarette, crushed it out in a saucer, and wondered what all the years of graduate studies and post-doctoral work had gained her when it seemed in times like this she could barely participate in her native language. "You're angry at me about something, Olivia. Why don't you tell me and get it out in the open."

"You wouldn't understand."

Ah, the fall-back position of every child. Well, she had a mother-fall-back response of her own.

"Try me."

"You'll get defensive."

"No, I won't."

It was then Beluga realized that she had fallen for the universal mother-daughter conversation. The rhythm of this, the very patter, had to have been recorded in molecules and tucked into every pre-natal vitamin supplement swallowed all over the world. This potential for fruitless interchange grew within the mother and was transferred to the child like some form of time-released DNA.

Then, at just the right moment, or more likely the wrong moment, the inevitable conversation popped up. If there was a molecular half-life when Beluga could be sure the threat for circular arguments was waning, no one told her. She just hoped she'd live long enough to see it.

"Talk to me, Olivia."

"I'm surprised your *insight* hasn't figured it out."

Aha! Now they were getting somewhere. "My insight has been remiss in meeting your needs?"

"Damn right."

"I'm sorry. Really I am."

"Why couldn't you be a normal mother?"

"Tell me what one is, and I'll try."

Olivia bounced out of bed and paced around the room. "Encouraging me in dance classes, cheerleading, you know. Things like that."

"Honey, you hated those things."

"You never even made me breakfast."

Beluga could barely conceal hurt and defensiveness. "I always fixed it for you on the first day of school."

"Yeah," Olivia said with disgust. "And the last time was when I was in the sixth grade."

"You said you didn't want breakfast anymore. I

remember that much."

"And do you remember why? You gave me food poisoning, that's why Mother. I was sick for a week."

"It was an accident."

"I can't eat fried eggs and bacon to this day, thanks to you."

"They're overrated anyway. Pastry is more filling."

"It was the thought and your effort that was lacking."

"Look, I can only be who I am. I'm sorry if I wasn't who you wanted me to be, but I did the best I could." Beluga leaned forward in bed. "I loved you through diapers, pimples, two years of those abysmal proms, and your senior superlative of 'best kisser.' Which, by the way, still sends fear through my waking consciousness every time I think about it. I loved you through trips to every part of the world I could afford to take you or send you. Not to mention the small fortune I invested in Girl Scout cookies."

Beluga was on a roll. Much as she wanted to stop, she was powerless to do so. "Every stray you brought home was welcome. Every unnaturally colored powdered drink you wanted to consume was prepared. And there were so many visits to the emergency room that we were known on a first-name basis by the housekeeping staff. My heart sank when you brought home the FBI wannabe who wouldn't take off the coat with the epaulets if he were stranded in a desert. Do you remember he wore mirrored sunglasses in the dead of night? To this day, I wonder if he had eyeballs. And my heart soared when you pulled the graduation tassel from one side of your cap to the other and walked across the stage, a beautiful, sophisticated, young woman ready to change the world with her honors degree."

Beluga took a deep breath, released it slowly, and reached for a cigarette she never lit. "And somewhere in all of that, I fooled myself into thinking I would always listen to you and never go off on an unchecked, tangential diatribe like I did right now. And boy, do I hate myself."

Olivia stepped forward into the warm light and looked at her mother. The corners of her lips curled into a hint of a smile. "Every ten minutes during the movie, he called in to see if he'd been given an assignment."

"The FBI guy?"

"Yeah. And afterwards, he tried to impress a nightshift security guard with his credentials."

"Did it work?"

"The security guard hawked up a wad of chewing tobacco on his FBI spit-shined shoes. The guard said it was an accident. I thought it was a metaphor myself." Olivia grinned.

Beluga smiled, then burst into uproarious laughter that brought tears. She patted her chest, coughed, then settled to occasional snickers and, finally, thoughtful silence. "Olivia, all of this was a convoluted way to say I've loved every precious minute of you. And while I wasn't a mother in the classic sense, whatever that is, I will do it over and over and over again until I get it right if that's what you want."

"That would be some feat. If anyone can do it, it would be you." Olivia sat on the edge of the bed and took her mother's hand. "I love you, Mom."

"And I love you. Great, gooey gobs of it."

"I know it's been hard. Being a single mother and all. Then going back to school to get your doctorate after Dad died." She laughed self-consciously. "I barely remember him, but I still miss him."

"Me, too, baby. Me, too."

Olivia stroked Beluga's hand. "You know what?"

"No. What?"

"Maybe I did change the world with my honors degree. A little part of it anyway."

"Is that where you were these past two years?"

She nodded. "I was in a small village deep in South America."

"Uh, huh."

"Teaching kids to read. No electricity, no running water, and plumbing were only a far-future theory. Some of those kids had never even seen the ocean."

"But you taught them to read."

"And maybe opened a few doors through the words. I don't know. It seemed the thing to do. When all was said and done, I think I learned more than they did."

Beluga grabbed her daughter and held her tight. "I've never been prouder in my life. Your father would say the same thing if he were here. I know he would." She kissed Olivia on her head. "But for the record, if you ever go off again without telling me where you are, I'm calling the FBI guy."

"Is that a threat?"

"It's a promise, honey."

"I'll never do it again. Cross my heart and hope to eat a gallon of ice cream."

"Oooh." Beluga groaned. "That sounds good. Let's see if we've got any." She threw back the comforter and walked to the kitchen, followed by Olivia. "Wait. What am I thinking? The refrigerator gave up the ghost. Oops. Poor choice of words."

"I've been thinking about that too, Mom."

"And all this time, I thought you were off the case."

Beluga pried open one cabinet after another in search of a satisfying sweet.

"A daughter takes quality time with her mother when she can."

"What about letting the police handle it?"

"I think they've missed the scent. Or at least not sniffed it all out."

"Spoken like a true bloodhound, dear. There must be something to eat around here." She spied a package of iced oatmeal raisin cookies and pounced on it.

"The strange occurrences all center around the soundstage. But the proximity of the events to the office in that building, not to mention the very real events that have taken place in the office itself, are all rather pointed."

Beluga offered the one cookie that remained in the package to her daughter.

"I'll go halfsies with you." Olivia nibbled her share of the cookie.

"So, what's your theory?" Beluga asked after devouring her cookie piece in one bite. "I'm famished. And there are no more cookies."

Planchette jumped to the kitchen table to nose through the open script.

"Cats. Cat food. Hey. How does kitty kibble sound to you? Protein."

"I'm still working on a theory."

"It's a seafood medley," Beluga said, waving a small bag of cat food at Olivia. "Believe me; it sounds better and better all the time."

Olivia sat at the table and thumbed through the film script. "The police would never go for this line of thinking, and I can't believe I'm thinking it myself, but maybe we need to check out the 'feminine energy' feelings you picked up in the film office. It's worth a shot since I don't know what else we can do." She rubbed her feet and stared at her toes. "Look at those blisters. It's from my new pumps, you know. When I finally get a job, those things will be history, and I'm back to wearing comfortable shoes like the men do."

Beluga stopped short, reaching into the cat food bag for a little pick-me-up. "Of course. That's one way to check it out."

"What?"

"This high heel thing has been nagging me like an insolent three-year-old. The pay-off, Chuck Masters, and a woman in high heels who happens to be in the local movie business and who drops off an envelope filled with cash. Right now, this picture *is* the local movie business. There's nothing else going on."

"So?"

"So Gig said she kept spare clothes in the screening room for business meetings that popped up now and then. That also happens to be the location of her only set of heels. And the screening room was where the first sighting of a sticky note appeared." She looked out the front window and the beginnings of dawn. "I think we ought to buzz on over there before people start milling around and see what we can find."

"And just how do you propose to get in, Mom?"

A sly smile crossed Beluga's lips. She grabbed her purse, spilled the contents across the table, and found them tangled in a hairbrush matted with cat fur. "Behold the keys to truth. Boley can use his spare."

"I'll be dressed in a flash."

"Look, Olivia." Beluga's eyes twinkled. She held up

a mangled granola bar pulled from the depths of her pocketbook rubble.

Chapter 21

Dawn's early light found the three of them huddled outside the door to the screening room where the film dailies had been shown and the prints were chosen.

Beluga shivered in the damp cold and cursed under her breath when one key after another failed to work. Her ample pocket book batted her constantly in the hip and added to her frustration.

"What is this?" she asked, incredulously. "A suitcase key? Why would anyone carry a suitcase key around with them?"

"I don't know, Mom." Olivia hugged herself tight and pounded her feet like a member of an Irish dance troupe. "It's freezing out here, and I think Planchette is stuck to the pavement. So will you be so kind as just to open the damn door?"

"There's no need using nasty language around your mother. My hair curls at the very word."

"Consider it money saved on salon visits."

"I use one of those vintage vacuum cleaner devices to cut my hair, thank you. Bought it a few years ago from a TV shopping channel. The investment has almost paid for itself."

"And it shows."

"Hasn't Boley ever heard of labeling keys?" she asked, pounding the lock. "I'd even settle for color-coding about now. Damn it. Damn it all."

"Shhh," Olivia droned, pointing to Planchette. "The little ones might hear that nasty language."

Planchette winked then moved closer to the door.

"Besides, Mom, no one labels their keys. People like us might take advantage of the information and attempt breaking and entering."

Beluga tried another key. "We're doing nothing illegal here. I am a bona fide member of both cast and crew. Besides, if one has a key, it's not technically breaking and entering, is it?"

"It still smacks of trouble. And at the least, it's probably unethical."

"Are you changing your mind about this case again?"

"Give me those things. I'll get us in if I have to break the door down."

"There's my baby."

"No wonder it wasn't working, Mom. You were trying the same key over and over."

"So sue me. My fingers went numb ten minutes ago."

Finally, a key slipped easily into the lock and turned. The three pushed into the dark building, where the temperature was little better than it was outside.

Beluga waved her hand over the face of the near-wall and flipped a switch. "Now, if we can find a thermostat, hope for survival is renewed. I'll check this side, and you go over there. Planchette, you stand guard. Sound off if you hear anything."

"No thermostat. Anywhere." Olivia shrugged and blew a cloud of cold air with her breath.

"I'll tell you one thing," Beluga said, "whatever Boley's paying to rent this place is way, way too high." She looked up and over and spotted the projection booth. "Over there. Let's take a look."

She and Olivia climbed the short staircase to a door and tugged. It was locked.

"Of course," Beluga muttered.

Olivia fumbled with the keys. Nothing. Not one of them would budge the lock.

"Great. Just great. Now, what do we do?"

"Have you got a credit card in that piece of luggage you call a purse?"

"Please, Olivia. Not the tired old credit card approach. That trick makes clichés look innovative. Besides, it's only done in uninspired movies by amateurs who don't know what else to do."

"Your point, Mother?"

"I'll get it."

She foraged around in the massive bag and found a cracked and peeling, fake leather wallet. The snap had long since turned loose and ineffective, and the side pocket holding assorted cards, receipts, and yellowed notes, was held together by one remaining, stretched thread.

"Let's see. Temporary driver's license, insurance card, land conservation membership, water conservation membership, an ice cream sandwich wrapper, an unreadable business card, donation receipts to animal organizations, and a Canadian coin probably from a soft drink machine."

A picture fell from the wallet and floated to the floor. Olivia picked it up and stared at it in horror. "Tell me this isn't what I think it is."

"Yes, dear. The Amazing Randi."

"In your wallet? He debunked everything you believe is possible."

"That's why I have a target drawn around his face.

Oh, here we are. It's a gold card to boot. Will that work?"

"We'll never know until we try." Olivia tucked the card down into the lock and turned the doorknob. "Slick as ice."

"It would seem you've done this before." Beluga waved her hand. "Don't tell me. Really. Ignorance is a much-needed bliss in this case."

Olivia stepped into the projection room and hunted for a light switch. Her hand hit a table edge. Following the edge, she caught the base of a goose-neck lamp, traced its shape to a small knob at the top, and turned it. A beam of light filled the immediate space and revealed a table cluttered with shooting script pages and personal notes written in an unfamiliar technical language.

Above the immovable furniture was a large projector that filled the glass window space that faced the screen on the other end of the audience viewing room. Below the desk was a pile of discarded film sections that coiled and twisted themselves around each other like intimately acquainted snakes.

Beluga began stuffing the film into her large handbag.

"Mom? What are you doing?"

"Maybe picking myself off the cutting room floor. Besides, it might be interesting to see what isn't used in the final version. Just consider me the keeper of archival material."

"I thought there wasn't going to be a final version."

"One never knows."

"This place isn't set up for film editing. It's a projection booth. Why would strips of film be here in the first place?"

Beluga considered this for a moment. "Beats me. But

now that you mention it, it does seem rather odd. You look for a stash of clothes and a pair of heels, and I'll take a little gander at some of this film."

Olivia found a penlight next to the script pages and began scouting out the room. She moved chairs and kicked boxes around in the tight space. "This place is a mess."

The goose-neck lamp and its tight beam might be just the thing. Beluga pulled a strip of film from her purse and held it in front of the light. She squinted, wished she'd taken her optometrist's advice to order bifocals, and stared at the tiny frames. "This is impossible. Is there something else I can use?"

Olivia stopped in her search and pointed at another piece of equipment. "Try that. If I remember it right, the light should be about here. Yep, that's it. Now thread in the film. There you go. Do you really need to do this now?"

"How did you know about this machine?"

"Film appreciation class. An elective sprung on me my last quarter. It was that or wrestling. But it turns out I ended up in a form of wrestling anyway since the professor particularly liked one-on-one with students in the dark of the editing room."

"He should be shot. And after hearing this bit of news, I wish you'd taken real wrestling."

"She was a great teacher, the wrestling part aside, and has since moved to another college. I hear she's settled down and quite happy. We all have lonely moments in our life."

"Tell it." Beluga groaned and stared into the machine that enlarged the film and ran it. "I knew it. My best side was gathering dust and footprints on the floor." She dug in her purse for another film piece, loaded it in the machine, and watched. Her mouth dropped open. "I don't believe it. Come see this, Olivia."

"What are we watching? That's Gig, isn't it? Who is she talking to?"

"Sanders Siler, the DGA spy. She said she didn't know he was in town until she saw the dailies, but there she is, talking to him. And look. Here comes the Bee Man into frame."

"But isn't that him flying in the air?"

"Yeah. It's some kind of special shooting technique. Now she's talking to both of them, and she doesn't look very happy."

"She's walking away."

The film stopped.

"Gig lied to me. She knew about Sanders Siler and the Bee Man all along. I can't believe she lied to me."

"Kinda makes you wonder what else she may be lying about, huh, Mom?"

"It most certainly does, sad to say. I like Gig. I like her a lot. But I am really disappointed, and a little scared. How are you doing on the search for her clothes?"

"Nothing yet."

"Keep going. I'll make a quick call to Tanya. I know there's a phone somewhere around here."

She found it buried under food wrappers and a mountain of script pages.

Then a larger, tottering pile of papers fell over and exhumed the note. A single smiley face peered up at her. The note scribbled under the face was signed this time. "Bingo."

"Double bingo. I found some clothes and a pair of heels over here."

"The smiley face note has Gig's signature. Put on the shoes."

"What?"

"Try the shoes and walk around. I want to hear them on the floor with a little weight in them."

"You try on the shoes."

Beluga scrutinized the heels her daughter held in her hand. "Darling, my toes wouldn't fit sideways in those shoes."

"And I'd have to bind my feet for a year to fit these."

"You're closer. Please, honey. For me."

Olivia sighed dramatically and removed her shoes and socks. With a painful grunt, she forced her feet in Gig's tiny heels and tramped around the small, available space.

"No, baby. You're not crushing grapes. You're on a tight schedule and dressed for success. Try it again. This time with feeling."

"My feet have lost feeling."

"Even better. Keep moving." Beluga closed her eyes and tried to match this sound with the one she heard while captured in the head mold. "It's no good. You can take them off."

"I think they're stuck." Olivia leaned against a wall and worked on prying them from her feet.

The shoe experiment was a bust, but all was not lost. In fact, things were beginning to fall into a logical, disturbing place with the discovery of the discarded film piece and signed sticky note.

Was Gig capable of murder?

Anyone was if the circumstances were right. And while it appeared that the Bee Man killed Sanders Siler, could Gig have killed the Bee Man? That was possible, but could she also shove him into an air vent?

And what about all the evidence found in Jett Blacke's destroyed trailer? Granted, it was circumstantial but greatly enhanced by the statement given to the police. Except no one knew for sure who gave the statement since that little bit of information had yet to be revealed. Still, there were the magazine cut-outs, the business card, and the large amounts of wire and latex.

Wire for garroting and latex for asphyxiation. All special effects paraphernalia used on a regular basis in low-budget horror films. But would they be lying around in great quantities in the star's trailer until they were needed?

No, that didn't make any sense. Not only would Jett refuse her trailer to be used for storage, she had nothing to do with special effects of any type. Her role, and personality, wouldn't have it.

It was a setup. And the supplies were used to set the scene for murder *after* the trailer was peeled by the Jaws of Life and hauled away. These were supplies used in a special effects business and, one presumed, readily available for the asking. Especially if the someone asked was in dire financial need and was offered a pay-off. Someone like Chuck Masters.

Beluga reached for a cigarette and lit it.

"No smoking, Mom. There's a sign."

"So I didn't see it. Besides, I need to smoke. It helps me think."

Gig knew Chuck Masters. As the director of this picture, she had to know all the players. The biggest threat to her had been the DGA spy, and he had been taken care of. That meant the Bee Man might have been in on the scheme. If the Bee Man made worse demands than Siler, would those demands force Gig to get rid of him? In light of the threats the surly hymenopterous actor made to Boley Ash, it was a possibility.

With the help of Chuck Masters and his special effects repertoire and her own developed skills in directing a good story, Gig could indeed stage a scene of murder. And who better than the hateful Jett to take the fall?

The question still remained. Could Gig kill the Bee Man?

Beluga took a deep drag from the cigarette then stuffed the film and sticky note in her purse. Yeah, it was definitely possible. "It doesn't look good for Gig. Not good at all. Ask me if I hate it."

"Do you hate it, Mom?"

"I hate it a lot. Thanks for asking. Now, if you'll put those clothes back where you found them, I'll make a quick call to Tanya."

She picked up the phone, dialed Tanya's number, and waited through the inescapable and painful phone message recorded, along with ear-piercing mariachi music. Tanya rationalized that screening her calls made her a little less accessible and quite a bit more intriguing. Beluga found it all a colossal pain in the backside and tapped her fingers on the desk while she waited for the beeps.

"Tanya. Pick up the phone now, or I'll—oh, there you are. You were sleeping, weren't you? I can tell by the combination of German, Italian and English expletives. Your international vocabulary has really grown. Not for the better. What's that?"

She listened closely. "Now, there's an interesting bit of synchronicity for you. I want to meet with Gig, too.

She's where? Yeah, she said she'd head back to the soundstage in the morning. Okay. Huh? She's right here. Just a sec." Beluga turned to Olivia with the phone thrust out. "She wants to talk to you."

"Hi, Auntie Tanya. What's up?" Olivia fidgeted with a knot in the phone cord, then stopped suddenly and smiled. "That's great news." She glanced at her watch. "How long ago did he call? Okay. Got it, and thanks." She handed the phone back to her mother.

"This phone call is over now, Tanya." Beluga rubbed her belly. "Now that you mention it, I'm as hungry as an empty bull. Breakfast will be just fine." She nodded into the phone while rummaging through some crumpled food wrappers. Nothing. Not a bite left. She lit another cigarette. "Yeah, meet me at the soundstage. I might need some backup if things don't go well. See you there."

Olivia bent and kissed her mother.

"What was that for?"

"Squint, the nosy crime reporter, wants to see me ASAP. Seems he's got some secret news he's willing to share on the case. And he's set up a meeting with his editor for a job interview."

"Hasn't he already got a job?"

"It's for me, silly. Isn't that fabulous?" She stopped and looked at her mother. "Is it okay? I mean, you'll be all right in your meeting with Gig? Oh, maybe this isn't such a good idea. I'll call him and set up another time."

"You'll do no such thing." Beluga threw her handbag over her shoulder and headed down the steps. "Inherent coward that I am, trust me when I say I'll run like the wind if things get tricky. Besides, Gig's a nice girl. It'll be fine."

"Even if she's a cold-blooded killer?"

"There is that." Beluga hesitated briefly. "I've got my wits and intuition to set off alarms if I'm in danger. What more do I need?"

"The police?" Olivia locked the door to the projection room.

The outside door leading into the building rattled, then flew open with a clang. Planchette screeched.

"A little late with the warning, boy, but I knew you'd come through."

A uniformed security guard jumped back, then recovered himself by tapping a chewed pen on a clipboard. "I don't see no note here that says someone should be in the building about now."

"Well, we—"

He raised his hand to stop the conversation. His eyes narrowed as he looked from the clipboard to them and back to the clipboard. Lips curled back in an imperious grin sans the help of front teeth, he adopted his most official tone.

"Now's time for explaining. Who are you, and what are you doing here?"

Beluga pushed her daughter through the door, nudged Planchette out, and followed them. "We were just leaving."

"Whoa there, little lady," he said, grabbing her arm. "I asked a question, and I aim to get an answer."

Beluga stopped short and stared at the man's hand on her arm as if willing it to burst into flames. He released his grip and stepped back. Closing her eyes briefly, she summoned what information might be available to her.

"Petey wants the sergeant job. He's meeting with the boss right now to lobby for it. You might want to get over there as quickly as possible."

The guard was emotionless at first, then stared sightlessly at her. "Sumbitch." He spat a thick stream of tobacco juice on the ground. "I knew that Petey fellow would stab me in the back if I gave him half a chance. He's slick, that one. Slicker than snot on a doorknob." He turned on his heel and threw commands over his shoulder. "See that you get signed in next time. And lock the door before you go." He spat again. "Sumbitch."

"See?" Beluga said as the three walked to the car. "Not bad for a psychic investigator, huh? Touch me. I'm hot. Searing hot."

"You're hot, Mom."

"And right on the psychic mark. So tell them to bring it on. Bring it all on. Everything they've got."

Planchette's yowl came low and plaintive.

"It'll be a piece of cake now, Planchette. You'll see. And as easy as pie."

Chapter 22

Beluga and Planchette stood in front of the open door to the soundstage where Olivia had dropped them off.

The separation hadn't been without second thoughts and doubts on Olivia's part. Her offer to stay through the meeting with Gig rather than leave her mother stranded with a possible killer was offered in earnest. She had also been thoughtfully concerned about Tanya's lack of bodyguard skills in any language, breakfast or no breakfast.

Now that was mother-daughter love.

But Beluga had strongly declined the offer and watched as Olivia drove out of sight. Then headed directly toward the office, with Planchette leading the way.

Her intuition was on red alert.

Her stock of pastel cigarettes was ample.

All senses indicated this was a safe place for a meeting since there were no feelings of ghosts or further attempts at murder.

And even with the worry of Gig as a cold-blooded killer, Beluga was confident things would work out. They always had before. Most of the time. Usually. On occasion. No, she wouldn't allow doubt to color her current positive outlook. This time things would work out. She was sure of it. She was hot. She was on the psychic mark. She was at the door to the office, and nothing out of the ordinary would happen on this day. Or in this meeting.

Gig was waiting. The gun held in her small hand pointed directly at Beluga's head.

Planchette hissed as every hair on his body stuck out like a bottlebrush. Then he jumped straight up, landed on his feet facing the opposite direction, and dived under a chair.

Every muscle in Beluga's body tensed and froze in position. Her heart skipped a beat, another, then pounded in her chest like a well-greased jackhammer. With her mouth dried to dust, she couldn't have said anything if she wanted to. Even her teeth felt loose.

Slowly, ever so slowly, Gig lowered the gun and scrutinized the woman before her. "I like that one. Although I've never seen gladiolas in that color before."

Beluga's lips twitched. She would have stripped stark naked and handed her muumuu to the director if she liked it that much, and that's what it took, but right now, she could only manage a weak "Hunh, hunh."

Gig stroked the gun, then blew across the barrel. "Jett would have used this. She was looking forward to it as a matter of fact. But I guess that's water over the dam." She dropped the gun on the corner of the desk and started tinkering with the myriad collection of sound equipment that shared the table space.

Beluga called on what residual strength her shocked system could spare and launched herself at the table. Dropping short, she rolled hard against the table leg and knocked the wind out of herself. The gun tottered off the edge.

It took days, it seemed, hours at the very least, for the weapon to drop with an audible *thunk* next to her knee.

She grabbed it and aimed at the underside of the table. Then the wall. Then with a bend in her elbow like an experienced gunslinger, she aimed the gun at the ceiling. No other target was readily available, so she'd take what she could get.

Gig's face suddenly appeared over the table edge. A frightened Beluga dropped the weapon. It skittered under the table to stop at Gig's feet.

The director picked up the gun, came around the corner of the table to Beluga, and handed it over. "Look, if you want it that bad, it's yours. Makes no difference to me. It's not like I'll be able to use it now."

Beluga stared at the gun and tried to work feeling back into her jaw muscles. Easing half her face out from under the table, she peered up at Gig. "You weren't going to kill me?"

The director stepped back. "What on earth are you talking about?"

"The gun," she said, waving the weapon as irrefutable proof. "I thought I was a goner."

"It's a prop, Beluga. It makes a bit of a racket, but it shoots blanks. We add foley sound in later so that every fired bullet makes a blast like a cannon." Gig reached out to help Beluga up. "Even blanks at short range could cause an injury, a minor one, so I've been told, but it would hardly kill anyone."

Beluga brushed off her dress but held tight to the gun. Just in case. Gig had lied before.

"Why would you think I'd try to kill you?"

"I could ask you the same question, but I seem to be a little busy right now."

Beluga's eyes rolled to one side. A flush of heat started on her neck and traveled to her face.

Embarrassment touched her voice.

"I think it's safe to say my bladder was as tense as the rest of me. It's relaxed now. More's the pity."

Gig came around the table. "Look, I'm sorry if I scared you. But do you see all this?" She waved at the jumble of equipment gathered on the table. "I'm taking inventory and checking to make sure everything works before sending it back. Since the film is over and everything. The gun was just one of many rental items. Like the sound recorder, the script supervisor's camera, the boom mics. All this stuff."

Beluga took a moment to look around the room. Planchette had stayed glued to his position under the chair. His bottlebrush impersonation was gone, but his eyes stayed wide and alert. Then she noticed the office walls were back to boring white. "The sticky notes are gone."

"In the trash. It took me an hour, but I'm nothing if not fastidious about leaving things the way I found them. This film office included."

Gig was destroying evidence, sweeping away the remains of her tracks. But there was only one way to find out for sure. Beluga pulled the sticky note out of her purse and showed it to Gig at arm's length.

"What do you make of this?"

"Nothing."

"Nothing? Not a thing? It has your signature at the bottom."

"It has my name at the bottom, Beluga. But that is definitely not my signature."

"Why did you lie to me about Sanders Siler? I saw you talk to him and the Bee Man."

Gig's face paled. "When? Where?"

"It's all on film. Not the part we saw at the dailies, but the part that was cut before that scene was shown."

The director collapsed as if a plug had been pulled and released what energy she had left. "Yeah, I saw him, and I talked to him. It was on film? I never saw it."

Beluga scanned the equipment on the desk, zeroed in on the sound recorder, and pushed the button. "I'm sure you won't mind if I get this all on tape."

Gig shrugged. "If you must, for what good it'll do. It doesn't matter now. Siler is dead. The film is dead."

"You knew Siler was in town?"

"He called and told me. I told him to stay away. He wouldn't. It's as simple as that."

"A DGA spy called to tell you he was in town?"

"An ex-lover, who happened to be a DGA spy, wanted to rekindle old affections. He was off-duty and would never turn me in." Gig brushed away a tear and shored herself up with a deep, painful sigh. "Maybe if I'd been more assertive, Siler would have gone back to California. I can't help but feel responsible for his death."

It wasn't logical or practical, and it certainly didn't make for objective investigative work, but Beluga's heart went out to this petite woman.

"You didn't tell anyone he was here? Why?"

"It was a personal matter, none of their business. But they all knew why he was here anyway or thought they knew. The idea Siler was spying on me made the cast and crew pull together and work harder. So I didn't tell anyone. It seemed the best decision at the time."

"Do you think the Bee Man killed him?"

"I don't know. Your theory makes some sense. And Winchester Rainey, the Bee Man, was always working deals on the side. Drug deals, blackmail schemes, you name it."

"Delusions of grandeur."

"Yeah, and ego. I wanted him off the picture and said as much. He was not happy about it and tried to get Siler to do his bidding. Siler wouldn't bite, so the Bee Man threatened to go over his head. By that time, I was so disgusted with the both of them that I walked off. I wish I hadn't now." Gig twirled a pencil around her fingers and chewed her lower lip. "I can see why you thought I was trying to kill you. But I wasn't, Beluga. For what it's worth, I'm telling you the truth, and I hope you believe me."

"I don't know what to believe anymore," she said. "So while I'm sorting all this out, tell me why this meeting was called."

"What meeting?"

"Our meeting. You and me. I got a message I was to meet you here."

"I didn't call you for a meeting."

Planchette growled.

A tickle started at the base of Beluga's neck. "Then who did?"

"I did."

Beluga turned slowly in place as a chill crept up her spine. Gig maintained her seat and gave away her feelings only through a slight grimace.

Betty stood at the door. The gun in her hand pointed at Gig this time.

A smile formed on her lips. She licked them as if savoring something particularly wonderful. "It's getting better and better all the time."

The gun in Betty's hand had to be the real thing. No doubt it held real bullets, too. Beluga gripped the prop gun tighter in her hand and slipped it into the folds of her muumuu in case it was needed. Betty didn't need to know the prop gun held only blanks. In the meantime, Beluga opted for a diversion tactic to buy time for a plan. Light repartee had always worked before.

"I know the high regard you hold for your plastic surgeon. Believe me, it shows. But you don't need to put a gun to our heads for us to make an appointment." Beluga laughed, slapped her knee.

The sounds rang hollow in the room. So much for an ice breaker.

Amusement flickered across Betty's face. "Let's see how funny you are when you kill Gig."

"I'm sure you've mistaken me for someone else."

"I don't make mistakes."

"Like when you killed the Bee Man?" Beluga asked.

"Exactly like that. I have contacts, but he had more. And he didn't like to share. He also didn't like to follow orders. I really hate that."

"I'm not killing Gig or anyone else." Beluga stole a covert glance at the director.

Gig closed her eyes and seemed relieved at this news.

"Oh, but you are, Beluga. Then I'm going to kill you."

Beluga jumped to a spread-footed stance and aimed the prop gun at Betty. "Freeze." Her hands shook and wobbled it in small, erratic circles. "Now drop your weapon."

The words were a close approximation to every cop show she'd seen on television. Funny how stupid it sounded now.

Betty's aim at Gig never wavered. "She's dead any way you cut it. I can live with that, can you?"

No. Beluga couldn't. She could not have blood on her

hands. Not Gig's, not the previous victim's, and sadly, not even Betty's. The film editor caught Beluga's hesitation.

"Shoot Gig, and it'll all be over. Any question about Jett as the killer will simply be transferred to Gig. Trust me; it'll be my pleasure to take care of Jett all by myself. You will be a heroine for defending yourself from the real killer. It's perfect."

And it was. Perfect in ways Betty would never know about until it was too late. Beluga couldn't kill any living thing, that was for sure, but she could act the part of a killer like an Oscar winner. Beluga turned the gun on Gig.

"Please don't kill me," Gig pleaded. Tears poured from her eyes. She trembled. Then almost imperceptibly, Gig winked. "Do it, Beluga. Do it, *now*. Get it over with."

Beluga closed her eyes and started to squeeze the trigger. Please, please, please, let Gig know whereof she speaks. The blast reverberated in deafening tones. She gasped with the jolt. Gig and the chair slammed against the wall. The director's body slumped to one side, then fell to the floor with a sickening thump. She was ominously quiet. Too quiet.

"I killed her."

"Indeed you did, Beluga."

"No!"

A spreading pool of blood crept out from under Gig. "*I killed her*. It wasn't supposed to happen like this. It wasn't…I…oh, dear God, help me. Help me. What have I done?"

Panic filled her; remorse weakened her. She dropped to her knees.

Gig had been wrong about the gun, and now the unthinkable had happened.

"She lied to me. Gig lied to me again, and now I've

killed her."

Beluga flung the gun at Betty, then sobbed and wailed with pain she didn't know was possible. A beautiful living creature had been killed by her own hands. Another soul had been released before its time. Cold-blooded killer was the right term, but now it applied to Beluga Stein, P.I.

"Call the police," she weakly said. "I have to turn myself in."

"No, my dear. It's not that simple. I have something else in mind for you."

Beluga looked up at Betty with tears running down her face. "There is nothing else for me."

"There is. Trust me."

Trust Betty? She couldn't even trust herself right now. But if she could get away to the police and tell them everything, then she could at least make sure Betty wouldn't be around to kill again. Beluga tucked her legs under herself and crawled toward Betty.

"No more. Just leave me here to die."

"My thought exactly. In fact, there's a beehive prop with your name on it. No air inside, but your name is on it just the same, at least to my way of thinking. What better place for a murderer to hide? So leaving you here to die is most assuredly my thought."

No doubt it was, and that wasn't good. Not good at all. Beluga looked at Planchette under the chair. Every hair on his body stood on end. He watched her every move without blinking. She nodded ever so barely. He crouched then. Muscles rippled under his sleek skin. His tail twitched in preparation for the command.

"Now!" Beluga shrieked.

The film editor fired. Her scream of pain punctured

the air as Planchette dug claws deep into the skin of her arm and bit with razor-sharp teeth. The gun flew from her hand, and plaster board exploded behind Beluga. She threw herself at Betty. Upon impact, the two women crashed out of the door and into a tangled heap.

With his teeth still firmly lodged in Betty's arm, Planchette turned his ample claws into a dervish of scratching that drew blood. She slammed her arm against the doorjamb then flung the stunned cat into a dark corner. He lay motionless.

"Planchette!" Beluga yelled.

Betty rolled out from under Beluga, jumped to her feet in an instant, and stood on one of Beluga's wrists. "I've had all I'm going to take from you." From her jacket, she pulled out a small narrow knife.

"You're hurting me."

"That means I'm doing it right. Even-steven."

Betty leaned over and raised the knife high in the air. It sparkled in the office light.

Then a vortex of wind forced Betty unnaturally upright as if pulled at the end of puppet strings. Yanked from her hand, the knife buried itself up to the hilt in a two-by-four leaning against the back of a set.

Betty bucked and danced at the wind's choreography, then staggered forward, deeper into the building. Her mouth formed an anguished scream that was lost in the ear-piercing howl of the supernatural storm born not from one but from three.

Beluga rose on one beaten elbow and stared in wide-eyed fascination at the scene playing out before her.

The thing propelled Betty forward, step after step. Peripheral air currents threw open a flap of latex to the beehive prop. With the help of three sets of barely visible arms, it guided her inside. Her knees buckling and arms thrust out, Betty resisted.

Beluga caught something in the corner of her eye. She shook her head as if clearing her mind would make sense of these events.

Gig's body, as if on its own set of puppet strings, rose slowly from the floor. Stumbling forward, she caught herself and staggered to the door. The front of her clothing was soaked in blood. Her face was neutral of any emotion, almost zombie-like as she watched.

The howling escalated to a sound that rattled the building walls and shook the ground underneath. It was rage in its purest form, but also something else.

Freedom, Beluga knew then. And for two anyway, justice for the wrongs inflicted upon them.

Betty was pushed into the beehive prop. A flap of latex snapped over the opening as if it never existed.

Then, as instantly as the supernatural wind appeared, it was gone.

Now a rhythmic wail off in the distance grew closer with every second.

Gig cocked her head at the sound. "The police. There'll be some serious explaining to do."

"You're alive."

"Yes, and not much worse for the wear. Although I expect we will be in a world of aches and pain tomorrow."

"Planchette!"

Beluga tried to stand, but her body refused to cooperate. She scooted toward him as best she could, then pulled her body along the floor with her good arm until she got to him. Cradling the motionless cat in her lap, she cooed at him.

"Oh, baby. My little one. My boy. It'll be okay. It will. It has to be." She gazed up at Gig with a tear-stained face. "He was my best friend."

Production Manager's Notes

Actress is out of jail.

Film editor is in jail.

Special effects man was offered immunity for his testimony. The IRS remains exempt from this deal.

Filming of Bee Mine is prematurely complete due to unforeseen circumstances. To wit: destroyed sets, unidentifiable food items from the snack cart debacle, incarcerations, supernatural occurrences, large people-swallowing props, and a cast and crew who have taken other jobs.

Director holds out hope of getting something in the can.

Beluga Stein holds doubt that will happen and was heard to say she had been wrong before. Not often. So rarely, in fact, that it's hardly worth mentioning. She has since gone home.

Beluga Stein's Diary

As hard as it is, I can rise above my ego and admit it. I was wrong.

A little time, distance, and advising freshmen on college career choices can bring new perspectives. So, I admit it. I was wrong.

Not bad wrong, but wrong in some definition of the meaning. So perhaps it was a good wrong since the movie was completed after all. And it is good, the film I mean, in a B-Movie kind of way. Or so I've heard. Soon I'll see for myself.

Gig called upon her ample talent to piece together the film in a way that made it work. Of course, it didn't hurt that she brought on a film editing wizard to help. A male this time, with no physical enhancements with which I'm aware. But then I leave those kinds of investigative duties to Tanya.

Some say our film is derivative of Robert Altman in style, with a touch of Ed Wood thrown in for good measure. But what the hey, who doesn't steal in the film business?

So tonight's the world premiere, and I can hardly wait. And instead of the cheesy apartment provided for me during the filming, Boley sprung for a lavish hotel suite. One night only, but it's better than nothing, which is more than I can say for the snacks in the suite refrigerator. Who thought granola bars and water were a good idea?

The party after the premiere is on me. All friends and family. This includes the cast and crew. Since they've become like family to me after our ordeal, they are welcome. It's going to be great.

Chapter 23

The phone rang and distracted Beluga from her diary. "Screen Actors Guild, IRS Branch. Just kidding. Beluga Stein speaking... Hi, Darwin. Yeah, constant ringing, right off the hook. You are coming tonight, aren't you? Great."

She looked around the room. "No, there's no surprise here, but pardon me if I say I'd rather not have any more surprises for a while if you get my drift... It's a nice one, huh? Okay. But I'm holding you to it. See you tonight."

Dressed in a gown of gorgeous green silk over satin, Olivia entered the room and put her hands on her hips. "I know you're not wearing that."

"This? Of course, I am."

"For once in your life, can you skip the muumuu?"

"I'll have you know this was custom-made just for the occasion. Rare orchids silk-screened on a vivid blue background."

"Mind if I put on my sunglasses?"

"In honor of the event, I'm only bringing cigarettes that match my outfit."

Olivia snorted. "I'll alert the media and the New York fashion designers."

Beluga poured two glasses of Champagne. "Have a drink with me? I'd like to propose a toast." She thought for a minute, opened her mouth to speak, and was promptly interrupted by the doorbell. "Hold the moment."

Her new high heels clattered across the marble floor. She pitched and yawed like a storm-tossed sailboat.

After throwing open the door, Beluga gasped at the size of the brown box the bellhop held. At least she thought there was a bellhop someplace back there. The only things visible besides the box were his legs underneath and his fingertips around the front edge.

"Please, come in. You can put that on the table here." Beluga stuffed a bill into the grateful bellhop's hand and ushered him out. She stared intently at the box. "Do you suppose this is the surprise Darwin just told me about?"

"Beats me," Olivia said, finishing her Champagne and reaching for a refill. "What are you waiting for? Open it."

"I think I will." She pulled open the top and tossed crumpled packing paper in a pile next to the table. "What the—?" Laughing, she dug deep in the box, shimmied the object out, then set it carefully on a bar stool.

"Please tell me that isn't you, Mom. Oh my God. It is you." Olivia circled the latex head warily then stopped in front. "What happened to your face? You look like you just sucked a lemon. Or the entire grove."

Beluga opened the accompanying note. "It's from Boley. He said he had to pay for it anyway and thought I should have it. And he thanks me for everything I've done, especially freeing Jett Blacke. So," she said, stroking the bald head, "Think I should donate my bust to the college library?"

"Your bust, yes. This thing, absolutely not." Olivia downed the Champagne and grimaced at the latex head. "Speaking of busts…"

"Yes, I heard about her in one of the dozens of calls today. Seems everyone wants to share the same news."

"And?"

"And it seems Betty was a little shaky on the details of the murders and less than forthcoming with information to the police as far as her involvement."

"But…?"

"I'd forgotten I turned on the recorder before she showed up on the soundstage. The police found it and used it to shake her memory."

"She confessed?"

"To the murder of the Bee Man, the smiley-face sticky notes, and masterminding the planting of evidence that set up Jett by paying off Chuck Masters. That is, she spilled all this after they brought in the prop beehive as evidence. One look at that, and she sang like a bird. I hear she still won't talk about how she got in there."

"Can you blame her?"

"It's hard to explain myself. It took a lot of fast-talking to convince them I didn't really plan to kill Gig, but I managed."

"It probably helped your case when Gig showed up to make her own statement."

"Yeah, I guess you're right. I'll never forget the pool of blood after I shot her." She shuddered. "It still gives me the creeps. Even knowing it was fake blood and Gig had palmed the stuff when Betty and I weren't looking."

Beluga lit a wardrobe-complementary cigarette. "And if things were fair, Gig should have shot me for suspecting her. You were right when you questioned the cut film on the floor of the projection room. Betty had personally staged that scene, figuring someone would eventually find the film, and the signed note, then sound off to the police."

"So, in today's myriad phone conversations, did

anyone say why Betty killed the Bee Man or why he killed Sanders Siler?"

"Yeah, as a matter of fact. It seems that—"

The doorbell rang again.

"Don't forget where we were while I get the door," Beluga said, tottering in that direction.

"As if I could, Mom."

Beluga opened the door to a huge display of wildflowers. The same set of bellhop's legs poked out from underneath. "Come in. You know where to go."

He ambled into the room, placed the large bouquet on the table, then spotted the head and jumped back a step.

"My alter ego." Beluga pressed another bill into his hand.

He nodded and, with a second, quick glance at the head, left.

"I hope that's it for the deliveries or I'll have to take a second job just to pay the tips. Unlock the door, will you, honey? That way, I won't have to answer it and break a hip when I fall off these shoes."

She rummaged among the foliage, found the card, and opened it. "How sweet. It's from Darwin." Her eyebrows rose to her hairline. "This must have set him back a month's pay. He shouldn't have done it."

"But he did, Mom. Why?"

Beluga glared at the door, expecting it to ring and destroy her chain of thought again. "Okay, but I'll make it quick."

"Please do."

"Forensics showed that Sanders Siler was given an overdose of cocaine. Enough that he could be suspended from an SFX crane without a fight. The drug affected his breathing, and so did a lack of air in the sealed costume."

Beluga decided to change her shoes. Let someone else wear high heels. She rummaged through her suitcase. "The white powder, along with marks that matched the obstinate crane's handle, was found on the Bee Man's hands. Win Rainey, the Bee Man, was strong enough to work the machine by himself, being a bodybuilder and all. And he was also more than a little unhappy that he couldn't bribe Sanders Siler to get to the gold he envisioned awaiting him via special treatment and union contacts. It turns out the Bee Man was a union member, too."

She inhaled deeply, blew out blue-gray smoke, and chose a pair of high-top sneakers. "Sanders Siler had clout and a conscience. He also had a temper when he felt forced into doing something he knew wasn't right. We'll never know, of course, but I suspect the combination of Siler's personal attributes scared the Bee Man into thinking his career was over and forced him to take action."

"Betty knew the Bee Man killed Siler?"

"She knew. And she used it. Here were two people, perfectly matched in their need to control, but Betty got the upper hand with her knowledge of the murder. She watched it happen from a dark corner of the soundstage."

"And said nothing."

"*Nada*. The Bee Man started what he called 'the domino effect.' It was a plan to scare people into doing his bidding, mostly by magazine cut-out pictures. As he became less successful at that tactic and bolder, he stepped up the fear with direct threats to Boley Ash."

"That was a safe approach since Boley controls the checkbook and quakes at his own voice. Right?"

"Right. Betty knew how to play the game more

skillfully than the Bee Man and without remorse. It was that simple."

"Simple for her, maybe," Olivia said. "A major run-around for everyone else."

"Except Betty had one major flaw that ultimately undermined her plans. Jealousy."

"C'mon, Mom. You can do better than that."

"Sometimes truth is stranger than fiction. She was jealous of Jett's acting success. If you can call this movie, a few deodorant commercials, and the rare television bit part, success. I don't, but Betty did. Although I'm certainly proud of my work in this film."

"We all are, Mom."

"B-movie aside, I think I delivered an award-winning performance."

"You were saying…?"

"Betty had played second fiddle to Jett Blacke since they were kids, and she'd finally had enough. She had the Bee Man on the ropes, saw an opportunity, and insisted he take it. He balked at her demand to kill Jett, so she killed him then stuffed his body in the air duct. I saw enough of her physical strength the last morning in the soundstage to believe she could do it."

"Why didn't she kill Jett herself? She tried to kill you."

"Again, I can only guess. But maybe the idea Jett would be in prison for a very long time was more appealing than Jett dead. Jail skits pale in comparison to all the glitter of Hollywood in Atlanta."

The suite door exploded open.

"Yoohoo, sweeties." Tanya raised an arm high above her head, draped herself along the length of the doorjamb, and flipped a boa over her shoulder. "*Manh ah guh-ee hoonh*. I have arrived."

"I see we've moved on to yet another tongue," Beluga said.

"What language is it this time, Auntie Tanya?"

"Urdu, dear, of course. Your mother suggested it. It's really quite a musical language and catchy. Like me. Stunning, aren't I?" Boa feathers shook loose, floated in the air, and fell about her face. She gagged, coughed, and waved frantically to free herself from the suffocating plumes. Instead, she launched more, covering her like a parade-route chicken.

Stepping in the room under a foul cloud, Tanya slid the boa off her shoulder and flung it over the back of the couch. "Well, if that didn't turn out to be the most disgusting, vile thing I've ever experienced."

"I assume you're referring to the boa," Beluga droned. "And not that sad display of Forties' cinema posturing."

"*Pila eik runh hay*. Yellow is a color. Unlike whatever hue you're covered in." Tanya scowled at Beluga's outfit. "You may speak to me when you're dressed for a world premiere and not a two-drink-minimum Don Ho show followed by mud wrestling. Wait a minute. I've got it." She grabbed one end of the boa and dragged it behind her in an exaggerated stroll. "That's it. That's the look I want tonight."

"A look I hope never to see again, by the way."

Tanya blew a raspberry and carefully stroked the boa before she replaced it over the back of the couch. "At least it was expensive. That has to count for something."

"Poor taste?" Beluga asked.

"You look beautiful, Auntie Tanya," Olivia said, with a look of warning aimed at her mother.

"Thank you, dear, as do you. And until I'm speaking to your mother again, you can tell her she's an old poot."

"Consider it done."

"Anyway," Beluga said. "Before I was so rudely interrupted by the fashion critic, I wanted to tell you why the flowers."

"They're for me, aren't they?" Tanya asked.

"Contrary to everything in your world of fantasy thinking, the flowers were sent to me. I clued Darwin in on some tests he could run to close this case. My star student did better than I could have ever hoped, and he got a raise for the effort."

"Maybe you didn't do so bad either." Tanya winked. "I hear the ME himself is coming tonight. He wants to see you. *Mera nam matchmaker hay*. My name is matchmaker."

"I thought you weren't talking to me."

"I'm not. It's just small talk to no one in particular."

"Small talk from a big mouth."

Tanya pursed her heavily fire-engine-red lipsticked mouth into a pout. "See if I ever pull your pompous butt out of the fire again."

"What are you talking about?"

"Did you ever once wonder why the police came to the soundstage?"

"Now that you mention it..."

Tanya puffed up proudly. "I called them."

"Why?"

"A phone call I got. Strange, scratchy, kinda hard to understand. But it told me you were in trouble."

"It?"

"I don't know how else to describe that voice."

Beluga smiled then. "I think I know that voice. I

234

talked to it on a phone that wasn't connected. It was the voice of reason, of guilt, anger, and frustration, and the voice of love. It was the manifestation of all that occurred in that soundstage. Good and bad. Fortunately for us, good won."

"Was it Boley's manifestation, Max?" Olivia asked.

"Partly. But it was also Sanders Siler and the Bee Man. All three lost souls looking for a little justice. Max tried to warn us the first time with the boom falling on the Bee Man. Then there was the fire, the electrical wires around Jett's legs, and the arrow-shaped display of papers that pointed at the air vent. All three eventually united in a single supernatural display to show us what was happening and maybe to prevent future injustices. It just took us a while to understand."

Aghast, Tanya looked at Beluga. "Are you telling me I talked to a ghost?"

"There are worse things, Tanya."

"I would prefer not to think what that might be. Unless it's more dresses in your closet like the one you're wearing."

"A toast," Beluga said. She poured glasses all around and produced one small bowl of tuna. "C'mon, Planchette. You've milked your recovery long enough."

A handsome cat face and sleek body appeared from behind the couch to join the gathering. His limp was barely noticeable. The boa feathers in his mouth were far more obvious.

"Planchette!" Tanya shrieked and chased him around the couch. "Come back here, you feline cretin. And if you cough up anything, it better be cash for a new accessory."

Beluga held up her glass and grabbed her daughter in a hug. "To family and friends, here and beyond." She sipped, then grinned. "And to the ME, the old goat. May you find out tonight just how much you missed me."

"Yet another performance?" Tanya asked, pulling the naked boa around her neck.

"The best kind of performance." Beluga winked.

For a while, at least, her imaginary gorgeous male companion could take some time off. He deserved it.

And so did she.